P9-AZX-340

Alice In-Between

BOOKS BY PHYLLIS REYNOLDS NAYLOR

Witch's Sister

Witch Water

The Witch Herself

Walking through the Dark

How I Came to Be a Writer

How Lazy Can You Get?

Eddie, Incorporated

All Because I'm Older

Shadows on the Wall

Faces in the Water

Footprints at the Window

The Boy with the Helium Head

A String of Chances

The Solomon System

The Mad Gasser of Bessledorf Street

Night Cry

Old Sadie and the Christmas Bear

The Dark of the Tunnel

The Agony of Alice

The Keeper

The Bodies in the Bessledorf Hotel

The Year of the Gopher

Beetles Lightly Toasted

Maudie in the Middle

One of the Third Grade Thonkers

Alice in Rapture, Sort of

Keeping a Christmas Secret

Bernie and the Bessledorf Ghost

Send No Blessings

Relunctantly Alice

King of the Playground

Shiloh

All but Alice

Josie's Troubles

The Grand Escape

Alice in April

The Face in the Bessledorf Funeral Parlor

Alice in-Between

ALICE IN-BETWEEN

PHYLLIS REYNOLDS NAYLOR

A JEAN KARL BOOK

ATHENEUM 1994 NEW YORK
MAXWELL MACMILLAN CANADA
Toronto
MAXWELL MACMILLAN INTERNATIONAL
New York Oxford Singapore Sydney

Atheneum
Macmillan Publishing Company
866 Third Avenue
New York, NY 10022

Maxwell Macmillan Canada, Inc.
1200 Eglinton Avenue East
Suite 200
Don Mills, Ontario M3C 3N1

Macmillan Publishing Company is part of the
Maxwell Communication Group of Companies.

First edition

Printed in the United States of America

10 9 8 7 6 5 4 3 2 1

The text of this book is set in Berkeley Old Style.

Book design by Patrice Fodero Sheridan

Library of Congress Cataloging-in-Publication Data

Naylor, Phyllis Reynolds.
Alice in-between / Phyllis Reynolds Naylor.—1st ed.
p. cm.
"A Jean Karl book."
Summary: When motherless Alice turns thirteen she feels in-between, no longer a child but not yet a woman, and discovers that growing up can be both frustrating and wonderful.
ISBN 0-689-31890-1
[1. Single-parent family—Fiction. 2. Family life—Fiction.]
I. Title.
PZ7.N24Ak 1994 93-8167
[Fic]—dc20

To my sister Norma, who knows why,

and to Colby Rodowsky,

one of my favorite authors

CONTENTS

ALICE
IN-
BETWEEN

1

ON THE ROAD TO RAVING BEAUTY

Aunt Sally said it happened to her, and to my cousin Carol. Dad said it happened to Mom.

"The summer between seventh and eighth grades," he told me, "was when she really blossomed into a beauty. You can tell by her photos."

I was eating crackers and cheese at the kitchen table, and decided I couldn't wait for blossoms (leaves, petals, anything at all) to unfold. I wanted to be a beauty *now*. Not that I hadn't been developing all along, but there wasn't any *name* for what I was at the moment. I certainly wasn't a child, but I wasn't a shapely teenager, either. Aunt Sally said that, sometime after your thirteenth birthday, you look in the mirror and see a woman. Which was nice, because my birthday was less than a week away. I wondered if there was any resemblance to Mom in me.

"Lester," I said, going into the living room, where my twenty-year-old brother was sprawled on the couch. "Look at my face and tell me what you see."

Lester opened one eye. "Cheez Whiz on your chin," he said.

I rubbed one hand across my mouth. "Take a really good look, Lester! Study my whole face. Who do I remind you of most?" I sucked in my cheeks slightly to make my cheekbones more prominent.

"Daffy Duck?" said Lester.

One of the problems of growing up without a mother is that there's no one around who has any idea what it's like to be a girl. For me, anyway, because I don't even have sisters. Mom died when I was four, and ever since, I've had to pick up all my information about being female from my aunt and cousin and friends at school.

Dad was writing checks in the dining room that night at the folding table he uses for a desk. And suddenly he said, "May ninth already? Your birthday's this Saturday, Al!" My name is Alice McKinley, but he and Les call me Al, which is what happens when there are only men in your family.

"You remembered," I said.

"Of *course* I remembered! Thirteen is pretty special, isn't it? Do you want a party?"

A few weeks before, I might have said yes, but I was thinking about the birthday party we'd just given Dad to celebrate his fiftieth, and I decided that one disaster was enough. "Just Pamela and Elizabeth," I said, naming my two closest friends at school.

"You got it," said Dad. "We'll order in some Kentucky Fried or something."

Pamela'd already had her thirteenth birthday, and Elizabeth wouldn't be thirteen till fall, but somehow I had the idea that by the time eighth grade began in September, we'd all be raving beauties. When I told Lester, he said, "*Raving*, anyway."

The day before my birthday, I wondered if Miss Summers would say anything to me about it at school. Sylvia Summers is my language-arts teacher, who's been dating my dad since December, only they're not having sexual intercourse, because I already asked Dad about it. At least they weren't when I asked, but Dad said I couldn't ask again, which means anything at all could happen. Except, knowing my dad, nothing's happening. Dad believes in long, slow courtships, and I worry sometimes that he'll let her get away.

Miss Summers has light brown hair and blue eyes, and on that day she was wearing an orange-and-white-print dress with a wide orange belt, which made her waist look really tiny. If Dad had told her my birthday was coming up, though, she didn't say anything, and I guessed that maybe Dad wanted to keep the celebration private—just between us and Lester and my two best girlfriends, which was okay with me.

"We'll be on our poetry unit until the end of the semester," Miss Summers told the class, "and I'd like each of you, in the weeks ahead, to memorize a favorite poem and recite it to the class—a poem that has special significance for you. I want you to recite it in a way that we can see your enjoyment of it. Take your time, and let it be a poem that really speaks to you personally."

My first thought was that maybe I'd do something funny, like "The Cremation of Sam Magee," but then I looked at the empty seat in front of mine and thought, No.

Ever since Denise Whitlock stepped in front of an Amtrak train, the whole school has been on "suicide watch." Nobody came right out and said it, but we heard that the faculty had been told to watch for students who were preoccupied with thoughts of death, or seemed sad or withdrawn, or were going through a crisis at home. I decided that any poem with *cremation* in the title might get me on the list.

"Suicide watch!" I would say to Pamela when she came to school dressed all in black. (Pamela does that; sometimes I look at her and think she looks sixteen. Seventeen, even).

Or the day Elizabeth had cramps so bad she was crying. "Suicide watch!" we told her. You kid around because you don't know what else to say. About Denise Whitlock and what she did, I mean. Sometimes it really hurts to think about all the kind things you could have said or done for her, but didn't.

When we got on the bus to go home that afternoon, Elizabeth was just about to sit down beside me when Patrick, who is sort of a special friend, slid onto the seat first. Elizabeth had to sit with Pamela, who had the second button of her shirt undone, and Elizabeth has told her a hundred times that she won't be seen in public with her if she leaves that second button undone.

"Happy birthday," said Patrick, and handed me a little box.

I stared. "It's not till tomorrow."

"I know, but go ahead. Open it!" he said.

I remembered the Whitman's chocolates he'd given me on Valentine's Day, and the Milky Way bar in sixth grade, and the chocolate-covered cherries. I figured it had to be something chocolate, but I was wrong.

Pamela and Elizabeth were watching from across the aisle when I took off the paper and found a small, rectangular box in gray velvet. It didn't look new, though. In fact, it looked sort of dusty. When I opened it, I found a gold bracelet with dark red stones in it.

"Patrick!" I said, surprised and shocked.

He smiled. "Do you like it?"

"Well, I . . . of course! It's beautiful, but . . ."

It looked very expensive. I don't know how I'd know, because I've never had any jewelry that cost more than $19.95. It looked like the kind of jewelry Miss Summers might wear, I guess. But it was really weird to be riding home from school on the bus and opening a velvet box with a gold bracelet in it from a guy who used to be my boyfriend.

I also noticed that there weren't any tags on it.

"Don't worry, it didn't cost me anything," said Patrick. And when I raised my eyebrows, he said, "It's Mom's, but she never wears it."

"Patrick!" I said again.

"It's *okay*!" he insisted. "She doesn't even like it."

I wondered if Patrick would ever look back on all the stupid things he's done and feel embarrassed the way I do when I remember mine. Or do boys worry about things like that? The only people who do dumber things than seventh-grade girls, I decided, are seventh-grade boys.

"You gave me your mother's bracelet, and she doesn't even know?" I squeaked.

"If she ever misses it, I'll tell her," said Patrick.

"No, you've got to tell her first. Patrick, if she ever sees me wearing it, she'll think I stole it!"

I could tell by his face he'd never even considered that possibility. "Okay," he said. "I'll tell her."

I wasn't in the house five minutes before the phone rang.

"Is this Alice?" came a woman's voice. "This is Patrick's mother, and I'm afraid he's made a terrible mistake."

"I know," I said. "You can have the bracelet back. I didn't wear it or anything."

"It's not that I don't want you to have it, dear, and I'm sure Patrick is very fond of you, but that bracelet belonged to my mother. And even though I don't care to wear it anywhere, I do feel it should stay in the family, don't you?"

"Sure," I said.

"Patrick is on his way over there now. I'm so sorry, Alice, but boys sometimes do things without thinking."

I had barely hung up when Patrick rang the doorbell. I had the gray velvet box all ready to go.

"Here," I said, but when I gave it to Patrick, he handed me another present. This was getting ridiculous.

"What's *this*?" I asked suspiciously.

"Happy birthday," said Patrick again.

I opened the package to find a can of Old English Lavender talcum powder, about the same time I noticed that the wrapping paper had *Happy Mother's Day* in pink in the background.

"Patrick?" I said.

"It was going to be for Mom, but I gave her something else instead," he explained.

"Well, thanks a lot. It smells really nice," I told him, and sprinkled some on each wrist. I *think* you're supposed to put talcum powder on your feet and armpits, but I figured Patrick wouldn't know the difference.

When Pamela and Elizabeth came for dinner on Saturday, bringing me a shirt and matching socks from the Gap, Pamela sniffed and said, "What are you wearing, Alice? You smell like my grandmother."

It was a good dinner. Dad brought home some fried chicken and a chocolate layer cake from a bakery, with mint chocolate chip ice cream to go with it, and a gift certificate from Woodward and Lothrop. I opened a card from Aunt Sally and Uncle Milt, which was an invitation for me and my two best friends to spend a week in Chicago that summer.

"Pamela and Elizabeth too!" I squealed, and all three of us yelped. "You'll love it," I promised, thinking how we could spend some time with my cousin Carol, who has her own apartment, and was even married once to a sailor.

The only thing missing from my celebration was Lester. He didn't come until the very end, when we were having a second piece of cake. The minute he walked in, I could tell by the way his mouth fell open that he had forgotten all about my birthday, but he tried to fake it.

"Don't tell me the party's already begun!" he said, and glanced at his watch. "Holy moly, not seven-fifteen! You mean you're celebrating without me?"

"I believe you know what time we generally eat dinner, Les," Dad told him.

"He forgot my birthday, as usual," I said.

"Forget? Me?" Lester pretended to look shocked. "How could I forget your big day?"

"Easy."

"You think just because I'm not carrying a present I didn't come prepared?" he went on, as full of baloney as a submarine sandwich. "I'm carrying your present in my head, Al. We've got a date, you and I. Your choice. You choose the time and place. Bowling? Movie? McDonald's? A whole evening just with you."

I looked at Pamela and Elizabeth. They knew he was full of baloney too, but we weren't about to let him off the hook.

"I want to go to a play at the Kennedy Center," I said.

I saw Lester swallow. "You got it," he said.

"And I hear that the Watergate has some great restaurants," said Elizabeth.

Lester stared at Elizabeth, then at me.

"That's it!" I told him. "First dinner at one of the Watergate restaurants, then a play at the Kennedy Center."

"And then he's got to take you dancing," said Pamela.

"Now wait a minute," said Les.

"That's it, Lester! That's my choice, my big night out, my evening just with you! Dinner at the Watergate, a play at the Kennedy Center, and then dancing. It's wonderful! Thank you so much. One of the nicest presents I ever had," I told him.

Lester looked at Dad, as though he might get him out of it, but Dad just smiled. "Enjoy," he said.

"Okay," said Lester. "When will it be?"

"A week from tonight, or whenever you can get tickets," I said.

"Wearing your best suit and tie," added Elizabeth.

"Happy birthday, Alice," said Pamela. "This could be the start of something big."

2

In the Fast Lane with Lester

It was after I went to bed that night that I began to worry about Miss Summers and my dad.

Elizabeth and Pamela had stayed till late, and we all sat around our oversized coffee table in the living room, talking about whether we wanted to fly to Chicago that summer or take the train. Lester went to bed early with a headache, and after the girls had gone I lay in bed smelling the scent of sweet May flowers through my window, and I suddenly wondered why Miss Summers *hadn't* been invited to dinner.

Maybe she didn't see herself as part of our family yet. Maybe she didn't see herself as part of our family at all. Maybe Dad didn't see her that way, either. Perhaps she felt that if she celebrated one of my birthdays she'd have to celebrate them all, whether she was going with Dad or not. And then, the worst thought of all: Maybe she wanted Dad for a husband—a boyfriend, at least—but didn't want a daughter in the bargain.

Finally I couldn't stand it any longer. I got up in my green pajamas and went down the hall to Dad's room and walked back and forth a few times. I didn't think he'd been in bed very long, and sometimes all I have to do is make the floor squeak a lot and he calls out, "Anything wrong, Al?"

But tonight nothing creaked, so finally I tapped lightly on his door. There wasn't any answer at first, and I was afraid he'd been asleep. Then I heard a sleepy voice say, "Al?"

I went in and walked over to his bed.

"Anything wrong, Al?" he said, and lurched up on one elbow.

"I know I'm thirteen, and I . . ."

"Not yet you're not," said Dad.

"What?"

He scooted over so I could sit down on the edge of the bed. "You were born at eleven-forty-six on a beautiful May night, so you still have a half hour yet to go," he said.

"Well, I'm *almost* thirteen, then," I corrected, "and I suppose things like this shouldn't bother me, but I guess I would have liked Miss Summers at my party."

"She and I talked about it, Al, but were afraid that with Pamela and Elizabeth there, it might create talk around school that we'd just prefer didn't happen."

"Dad, people already know you're dating her," I said. "They've seen you out together. They're *already* talking."

"I suppose, but there's something a bit more intimate when a woman is invited to family celebrations, don't you think?"

I didn't know how to tell him that people are wondering if he and Miss Summers are sleeping together, and he's only worried about what they would think if she came to my birthday party.

"I'm thinking it would have been fine with me," I said.

"Well, sweetheart, we're just not ready for that, I guess."

I tried to see his face in the moonlight. "Dad, tell me just one thing: Do you want to marry her or not? I don't mean tomorrow, I mean someday, maybe?"

"It's a nice daydream, Al, but there are too many things to consider right now, and I don't see that it's necessary to go over them all with you."

I gave a deep sigh. "May I ask you one more question?"

"Watch it, Al."

"Do you love her?"

This time there was a pause so long I thought maybe he'd gone to sleep. "I am very, very fond of Sylvia, let's put it that way. And I think . . . I *hope* . . . she's fond of me too."

I wonder who invented the word *fond*. It must be a cross between *like* and *love*, and I wasn't much for in-between stuff these days, seeing as how I was so in-between myself.

"Well, good night then," I said, leaning over to give him a kiss on the forehead. "Like me?"

"Rivers," he said, playing our little game.

"Love me?"

"Oceans."

As I started back across the floor, I said, "Was I born in a hospital?"

"Just barely," said Dad. "I thought for a while you were going to be born in our car, but I finally got your mother to the hospital, and you were born about ten minutes later."

"Did she . . . Was it painful?"

"Well, let's put it this way: She said she'd had worse days at the dentist's."

And just before I closed his door, he said, "Al?"

"Yeah?"

"You're thirteen now. On the dot. Happy birthday, honey."

The thing is, Miss Summers *did* remember my birthday. She sent me a card. *Happy Birthday to a Very Special Girl*, it said. And on the inside she had written, "I enjoy having you in my class, Alice. Sylvia Summers."

Was I special to her, I wondered? Did she really think of me—of Dad—as a big new part of her life, or only as friends in passing? I would have given up my big date with Lester just to be invisible for one evening to see what goes on between Dad and Miss Summers when they're alone. To hear what they talk about and see how they act toward each other. My friends had seen them holding hands in a restaurant. *I* hadn't even seen that!

About my date with Lester, though, Pamela and Elizabeth were more excited than I was. Probably because they've both had crushes on him for a long time.

"*We* are going to knock his *socks* off!" Pamela announced. "I've got this dress you're going to wear, Alice. It's black with this short, flouncy skirt and has big white polka dots all over. Mom got it for me to wear to my uncle's black-and-white wedding. You've got to wear it with black panty hose and tiny heels."

"I think we should fix her hair up with one of those big white ribbon barrettes—sort of sweep it up in back, with curls hanging down at the sides," said Elizabeth.

"And you've *got* to wear Obsession," said Pamela.

"What?"

"Calvin Klein's perfume. It makes men go wild."

"Pamela, I'm going out with my brother!"

"Well, other men around you will go wild," she said.

I wondered how a perfume did that, sorted out brothers from all the other men around you.

On Thursday of the following week, Lester told me he had tickets for a revival of *Porgy and Bess* at the Kennedy Center, and reservations at the Jean Louis (which is pronounced "Zhawn Looie," he said) before the show.

"You've got to dress up now," he warned me.

"I'm prepared," I told him.

On Saturday he went to his part-time job selling Maytag washing machines, and I put in my three hours at the Melody Inn music store, where Dad is manager. On the first floor are pianos and other instruments, with a big sheet-music department, run by Janice Sherman, the assistant manager, and the Gift Shoppe, run by Loretta Jenkins. Up on the mezzanine are little glass soundproofed cubicles where instructors give music lessons. My job is to do whatever Dad or Janice Sherman asks me to do, from washing the windows on the display cases to putting price stickers on sheet music.

Dad set me to work cleaning the glass on the revolving gift wheel in the Gift Shoppe, my favorite job. When you press a button, the wheel revolves and you get to see all the earrings and pins go around, all in the shape of instruments or musical notes.

"I wish I could find some really smashing earrings to wear tonight," I said.

"Big date, huh?" asked Loretta of the Wild Hair. Loretta is a year or so younger than Lester, and looks like an Aztec sun goddess, with her hair going every which way.

"With my brother," I told her, and explained how Lester had forgotten my birthday and was trying to make it up to me. Loretta, who's also had a crush on Lester from day one—unrequited love, as Aunt Sally would call it—really gets into the mood of things.

"These!" she said, choosing a pair of earrings that looked like dice, except that instead of little black dots, they had little black notes. The kind of earrings a woman would probably wear to a casino.

At four that afternoon, Pamela and Elizabeth came

over to help me get ready. Pamela was carrying her bouffant black-and-white dress, which looked like a skinny tube from the waist up, with huge puffy sleeves and a puffy skirt with a red flouncy pettiskirt beneath it, the kind of dress you might wear if you were doing the cancan on a stage in Paris.

Elizabeth had brought bubble bath, and after I'd bathed, they dabbed Obsession in my navel and between my breasts. (My "cleavage," as Pamela called it, except that it's hard to see a valley when there aren't any hills to speak of.)

Pamela did the makeup, because Elizabeth only wears lip gloss. She put on a moisturizer, foundation, cream rouge, then powder, eye shadow, eyeliner, mascara, lip liner and lip gloss. I hardly even recognized myself.

We heard Lester come home about 5:15.

"You through in the bathroom, Al?" he called through my door.

"Yeah, you can have it," I told him.

The hardest part was the panty hose. Elizabeth rubbed lotion all over my hands and heels so I couldn't snag them putting them on, but I had to take my hose off and put them on again three times before they felt right. I managed to make a small run near the top, but Pamela put fingernail polish on it to keep it from spreading.

When the stockings and heels were on, Elizabeth gave me a tissue to hold between my lips so we could slip the dress over my head. I couldn't even see myself in the mirror because Pamela and Elizabeth were hovering around me, pulling and twisting and flouncing and straightening, until at last the various layers of the dress fell into place.

"There!" said Pamela.

I stared. There stood a slim young woman in a puffy black-and-white dress, with sleek black legs.

They worked on my hair next, and by the time the big dangly earrings were swinging from my ears and my nails were painted bright red to match my heart-shaped lips, all I could do was stare.

"I don't believe this!" I breathed.

"I don't, either," said Elizabeth. "The real you! Isn't it amazing!"

You know what I wished right then? That Mom could see me. That I had a mother who would stand back and smile at me and say it was okay to look this good, this grown-up. I wouldn't even have cared if she'd said, "Our little moth has become a butterfly!" or something corny like that, because I actually *felt* like a butterfly.

Dad doesn't usually get home until after six on Saturdays, but I heard the door close downstairs and knew he'd come early to see us off.

"You ready, Al?" came Lester's voice from the hallway. "Soon as I put on a tie, I'm set."

"Almost," I said.

Pamela had brought over a small black purse for me to use, with Kleenex, comb, lip gloss, and stuff.

I turned around once more in front of the mirror,

noticing how my legs glistened in the silky black hose, and then Lester tapped on my door.

"Let's go, babe," he said.

I opened the door. Lester gaped. I mean, he gaped and gasped, both. Like people look on TV when they've just been shot in the heart.

"Wow!" he managed at last, and gave a low whistle.

Dad came to the foot of the stairs. "Everything okay up there?"

"I'm not sure," said Lester.

While Pamela and Elizabeth watched from my bedroom, I put one hand over Lester's arm and moved out into the hallway and over to the stairs.

A second gasp from below. Dad, at least, smiled as I came down, but Les was still in shock.

"Promise me just one thing, Al," Lester said. "Don't embarrass me, okay? Don't try anything big."

"I promise," I said.

I knew that Lester had thought the evening would be a big-brother-takes-little-sister-on-a-date kind of thing, when actually I didn't look very young.

"What I *mean* is," said Lester, "don't try to order in French or ask for wine or something."

"I don't drink," I said coolly.

"Right!" said Lester.

I saw him give Dad a helpless glance as we went out the door, but what *really* helped was Dad saying, "Al, you look beautiful!"

And I went grandly down the steps and waited for Lester to open the car door.

* * *

There was something about being with my twenty-year-old brother at the Jean Louis that was a lot different from eating dinner with Patrick at his parents' country club: At least one of us knew what we were doing. Lester translated the menu for me (*pâté de foie de volaille* was chicken liver pâté and *flambé* means that something arrives at your table on fire). He said it's considered sophisticated to order an appetizer whether you want one or not, but you can skip dessert as long as you have coffee. I would have liked to skip the appetizer and gone straight for the dessert, but I was glad Lester was teaching me things like that. So I ordered chilled avocado soup, which was gross, but Lester said I only had to take a few bites of everything.

"Are you finished?" the waiter asked me.

"Yes, thank you," I said.

"Very good, mademoiselle," he said, as though I had just finished all my peas and carrots, and he whisked my bowl away. I decided I liked eating in a place where no matter what you liked or didn't like or did or didn't eat was "very good" with the waiters.

It wasn't until dessert that I realized Lester was beginning to enjoy himself. Up until then he acted as though any moment I might pull the cloth off the table or trip one of the waiters or do something incredibly embarrassing. He was feeling so good, in fact, that he forgot how the evening was going to cost him an entire week's paycheck, and ordered us bananas foster, which is sautéed bananas over vanilla ice cream, covered with hot rum sauce.

We had parked at the Kennedy Center, so all we had to do was walk back across the street. But it was during the performance of *Porgy and Bess* that I blew it. I guess it was the woman singing "Summertime" in that clear, high voice that made me realize how much I was missing in not being able to carry a tune. I kept trying to tell myself that even if I *could* carry one, I still wouldn't be standing on a stage at the Kennedy Center singing, but that wasn't what was really the matter. I just felt weepy inside. Then Porgy sang, "Bess, You Is My Woman Now," and somehow I thought of Dad, finding Miss Summers to brighten things up, and at the end, when Bess goes off to the city with Sporting Life, I didn't think I could stand it. I used up two of the three tissues Pamela had put in my purse, and I could tell Lester was watching me warily out of the corner of his eye.

"Need another one?" he whispered.

"I dode theeg so," I replied.

By the time it was over and I had gone to the rest room and fixed up my face again, I looked okay. I took Lester's arm as we left the theater, and was the only one who remembered where we'd parked down in the garage, which got me extra points with Les.

I think he hoped I'd forget all about the dancing part. And I suppose, in a way, I should have, because I knew he'd spent a lot of money on me. But I also knew if I let Lester off the hook so easily this time, he'd probably forget my birthday again next year, and besides, I wanted the experience of knowing what to do in every possible situation. So when he said, "Well, Al, did you enjoy the evening?" I said, "So far, yes," and I heard him sigh.

"You don't really want to go dancing, do you?" he asked.

"Yes."

"In *that* dress? In those shoes?"

"In this dress, and in these shoes," I said.

So he took me to this hotel nightclub, where we sat at a little round table over by the wall and drank ginger ale. Finally he took me out on the dance floor during one of the slow numbers, me with my flouncy red petticoat peeking out from under my dress and my tiny black heels. We'd just taken a turn around the floor and were dancing back toward our table again, when we found ourselves looking right into the eyes of Crystal Harkins, one of Lester's old flames, who was dancing with a man of her own.

3

Rekindling the Flame

The number must have been just about over when we started to dance, because the moment we came face-to-face with Crystal, the music stopped.

"Well, well!" said Crystal, staring at me in astonishment, then at Lester.

"Friends, I presume?" said the man she was with.

"Why, yes," said Crystal. "Steve, this is Les and Alice McKinley."

The man looked us over. "Newlyweds, I'll bet."

And before Lester could open his mouth, I said, "How did you guess?"

Lester pinched my arm, but I could see Crystal's eyes laughing.

"They're the perfect couple, don't you think?" she said to Steve. And then, when the music started again, she told him, "Les is an old friend of mine, so I'd like a dance for old times' sake." And she turned toward Lester and put one hand on his shoulder.

Steve didn't seem to think that was such a great idea. But he said, "Sure, go ahead. I'll dance with Alice."

The thing is, I don't know very much about dancing, and Steve must have realized that because he soon gave up the fancy footwork and sort of moved back and forth from one foot to the other.

I realized it was the first time I had ever been in a man's arms other than my Dad's. Or Lester's. Patrick's put his arm around me, but he wasn't a twenty-five-year-old man who shaves. I looked over at Crystal and Lester, who were talking intently. Crystal was still as beautiful as ever, with her short red hair layered against her head, her smooth pale skin, and full bosom. I remembered when she had helped me turn a mess of a permanent into natural-looking curls. I wanted to look as mature and sophisticated in Steve's arms as she looked in Lester's.

"So how's married life treating you?" he asked me, holding me a lot closer than I liked. I had to tilt my head back to see his face. How did you talk and dance at the same time? I wondered. What if there was garlic on my breath?

"Okay, I guess," I told him.

"Only okay?" He laughed. It was about then I decided that women don't tip their heads back to talk to men while they're dancing; they sort of dance with their cheeks close together, and talk to each other sideways.

"That's better," said Steve, and held me closer still, grazing his cheek against mine.

The next time the music stopped, Crystal came over and took me by the arm. "We're going to the ladies' room," she told Steve, and before I knew it, she was pulling me through a dark hallway behind the bar and into a little wall-papered cubicle with a toilet in it. She locked the door.

"Listen, Alice, Les is going to help me escape. Steve is a real jerk. He's an octopus, with hands everyplace they shouldn't be. Somebody introduced us at another club this evening, and he's been following me ever since. I want to shake him so I can go home, but he gets mean when I try. Will you help?"

I had only been a teenager for one week, and already I was being asked to help out in the romance department. More than that, I might even be saving Crystal's life!

"Of course!" I said eagerly. "What do you want me to do?"

"Every time I've tried to leave, he's stopped me. So Lester said I could ride home with you, and then I'll take the Metro back downtown tomorrow and get my car. But we've got to sneak out the back way without Steve knowing."

I felt chills run up and down my spine and wondered if the octopus was outside the door listening.

"What you do is, go back to the table, and Steve will follow you to ask where I am. Tell him I'm still in the ladies' room, and ask him to get you another ginger ale or Perrier or something. When he goes to the bar, come back through this hallway and go out the exit at the end. Lester's going to have his car waiting."

This was the most exciting thing I'd ever done in my

life, next to being kissed by Patrick for the very first time.

I opened the door a crack and looked out. "He's there," I whispered.

"Okay," Crystal said. "Tell him I'll be out in a few minutes."

I opened the door and started back through the hallway, Steve the Octopus at my heels.

"Where's the redhead?" he asked.

"She'll be out in a few minutes," I said, leading the way back to our table. "Would you get me another ginger ale, please?"

He gave a short laugh. "Child bride, huh?" he said. "What'd you do? Marry at sixteen with your parents' consent?"

"You think I'm *sixteen*?" I said, trying to look shocked.

"Could pass for twelve, easy," he told me. And then, he simply snagged a passing waiter and asked him to bring another ginger ale to the table. *Now* what did I do? Crystal and Lester were waiting for me outside in the car. They wouldn't leave without me, would they?

"I like your earrings," said Steve.

"Thank you."

"You a gambling woman?"

"Not really," I said, beginning to feel very uncomfortable. I was watching the way his hand was moving across the table toward mine. I put my hand in my lap.

"Hey, not afraid of me, are you? Your husband disappears with an old flame, at least we can be friends."

"I think maybe I have to go to the bathroom again," I said, getting up.

Steve got up too, but he blocked my way to the bathroom. He put both hands on my waist, and turned me around toward the dance floor, pulling me right up against him. Suddenly I could feel one of his hands on my backside, and I wondered if Steve the Octopus was sprouting hands every which way. At that moment I heard Lester's voice behind me.

"Time to go, Alice," he said. "Nice meeting you, Steve. Take care." And then we were making our way through the dancing couples, down the dark hallway behind the bar, and out the exit door at the end.

Lester's car was parked right outside. "Get in," he said, and I slid in the front seat beside him as Steve came bursting out the back door and looked around.

"Hey, you see where Crystal went?" he called. "What's with the redhead? Where'd she go?"

"She said something about another appointment," Lester called out the window, and swung the car around in the parking lot, and out onto M Street. It wasn't until we were inching our way through Georgetown traffic that Crystal rose up in the back seat and we all broke into laughter.

"He was awful!" Crystal said. "I didn't think I would ever get away, Les. Thank you *so* much! You too, Alice, for letting me spoil your big evening. I'm really sorry about that."

"You didn't spoil it at all, Crystal. It was fun!" I told her.

"You should watch out for guys like that, Crystal," Lester said. "They can be mean."

"I didn't think you cared," she answered.

"Of course I care."

I leaned back in the seat and closed my eyes. There was so much to tell Pamela and Elizabeth I hardly knew where to start. I thought Lester would take me home first and then go off somewhere with Crystal to talk, but he didn't. He drove Crystal home, waited to see that she got inside okay, and then drove home with me.

"Lester, it's been a *great* evening!" I said. "I *loved* it. The dinner and the play and the dancing and rescuing Crystal and *every*thing! And you look so great in that suit."

"Well, you look pretty good yourself, kid. You're going to wow the guys, you know."

I was quiet for awhile. "Les, if you hadn't been there to help Crystal, what should she have done? What should I do if it ever happens to me?"

"Call home," said Lester. "Call home, and wherever you are, Dad or I will come and get you."

I think I really, truly, absolutely felt that Lester loved me right then.

It was sort of like Cinderella after the ball, I guess. Pamela had left some Pond's cold cream to wipe off my makeup, and it slipped right off. I got out of the dress with the bouffant sleeves and skirt, took off the dice-shaped earrings and the black panty hose and heels, and put on my green pajamas. When I looked in the mirror again, I didn't see the gorgeous creature I'd been at the Kennedy Center, but plain old Alice, with the same skinny legs, and wondered if this was the way all women felt—even Crystal and Miss Summers—when they got home from a date and took off the outer layers.

The phone rang, and I ran out in the hall and answered before it could wake Dad. It was Pamela.

"I'm over at Elizabeth's," she said. "We noticed your light was still on. Come on over."

I slipped my feet in my loafers, gathered up my clothes and toothbrush, and left a note on the kitchen table for Dad, in case he got up to see if I was home. Then I went across the street in my pajamas, and Elizabeth let me in. We tiptoed upstairs to her room, where they'd pushed Elizabeth's twin beds together, and all three of us crawled beneath the sheets while I told them about *pâté de foie* and dessert *flambé*, and how we had saved Crystal Harkins from the Octopus. It was exciting and scary both to think of all the things we were in for in the years ahead.

"What I wish," said Elizabeth, "is that after I'm married and the wedding night is over, I could come to your house and we could all talk under the covers, just like this."

"Elizabeth, after you're married you're supposed to talk to your *husband*!" Pamela said. *"Under the covers!"*

Elizabeth sighed. "Not like this, though. It would never be like this."

One of the things that was bothering Elizabeth, I knew, was the thought of ever being pregnant, because her mother was expecting in October. But I was getting sleepy, so the talk petered out. In the morning, we made our own breakfast because Mrs. Price can't stand to look at food at that hour, and then I went home.

But when I got upstairs, I saw the telephone cord stretched across the hallway and under Lester's door. I paused just long enough outside his room to hear whom he was talking to.

Crystal.

4

THE PENCIL TEST

I did something at school on Monday that I'd been thinking about since fifth grade but never thought I'd have nerve enough to do. I guess I was still thinking about *Porgy and Bess* and how beautiful it was when that woman sang "Summertime." And when Bess sang to Porgy, and Porgy to Bess, and all the street vendors were singing together. I wished I knew how it felt to be up on a stage singing like that—even in the back row of a chorus, where, when you opened your mouth and made a sound, people didn't turn to stare at you.

It was right after lunch when Pamela and Elizabeth and I were leaving the cafeteria to sit outside on the steps. We passed the chorus room, and I noticed the teacher standing by his desk, sorting through some sheet music.

"I'll meet you outside," I said to Elizabeth and Pamela, and ducked through the door.

I walked over to where he was working. I didn't even know his name. Maybe thirteen makes you bolder or something.

"Hello?" he said, smiling a little, and kept sorting.

"I'm not in chorus, but I've got a question," I began.

"Shoot." He was looking at me now.

"People say that when my mother was alive, she used to sing a lot. My dad plays the flute and piano, and my brother plays the guitar. They both sing too. I can't carry a tune, and don't understand it. I just wondered if it's genetic or something."

"Well, now," he said, and continued smiling, "it's probably a question no one has an answer for, but are you quite sure you can't carry a tune?"

"Trust me," I said, and explained how all through grade school, when the other kids sang for the PTA, I was given the triangle to ping at the end of each stanza. And when I sang "Happy Birthday" at parties, it brought down the house.

The teacher listened. "Well, some people believe in the Suzuki method, which goes on the theory that everyone can learn to carry a tune if they're exposed to music at an early age."

"I probably listened to it before I was born," I told him. "But I can't even tell you if notes go up or down."

He studied me a moment. "There are no guarantees, but if you really want to make the effort, I'd be willing to work with you each day for fifteen minutes and see what we could do. The real question, though, is how unhappy you are with yourself just as you are now. Would this make a big or a little difference in your life? Or no difference at all?"

I thought about that. Would I rather have fifteen minutes a day to sit out on the steps with Pamela and

Elizabeth after lunch and talk to the guys, or did I want to embarrass myself by trying to make my voice match the notes on a piano? And if I finally *did* get to the place where I could carry a tune, would I break into song when I saw my boyfriends coming toward me on the sidewalk?

"I guess maybe I'm pretty happy the way I am," I said finally.

He grinned. "Okay. If it ever bothers you enough that you feel genuinely unhappy about it, come back and we'll see what we can do. If it's only a mild annoyance, you probably wouldn't want to spend the time and effort."

I went outside smiling. I think it was the first time in my life that a teacher told me I could survive without knowing his subject. That I could live a long, healthy life and still not know diddly about what he was teaching. Maybe when you were thirteen, people treated you more grown-up. Maybe I *was* on my way to womanhood, and people could see it already in my face.

I told Dad that night what the teacher had said. "I hate to admit it," he told me, "but he's right. There was a time I fantasized that my children would be musicians when they were grown. Career musicians, I mean. And now I realize that if you were anyone other than who you are, you wouldn't be the Lester and Alice I love, and I wouldn't trade you for the world."

And that was the second time in a week I'd felt really, truly, totally, absolutely loved.

* * *

As the week went on, it got unusually hot for May, and when I came home from school on Thursday, Lester and Crystal were sunbathing in the backyard.

Lester had spread an old blanket on the grass and was lying on his back, wearing his sunglasses, his boom box playing beside him. Crystal was lying on her stomach in her bikini bottom and top, only the top was unhooked, and her back was bare.

I was noticing the *S* shape that a woman's body makes, from the small of the back and over the rise of her bottom. I wondered whether, if I was lying on my stomach and someone was watching me, *I'd* look that pretty. I don't think so. I wasn't as flat as an ironing board, but I didn't have hills and valleys either. Just a middle-of-the-road, in-between shape.

Lester and Crystal seemed to be talking to each other, and suddenly, right before my eyes, Lester sat up, reached for the suntan lotion, and began slathering it on Crystal's back. Only he didn't just slather her back. He rubbed it in good up around the neck and shoulders, and then his fingers slid around to the sides, *right next to her breasts,* and when he finished that, he rubbed the lotion *right under the top edge of her bikini bottom*.

Later, when Crystal had gone home, I said, "Lester, you sure get friendly in a hurry."

Lester took a long, slow drink of lemonade and said, "I haven't the slightest idea what you're talking about, Al. What are we playing? Twenty questions?"

"I saw the way you were slathering Crystal," I told him.

"*Slathering* Crystal? You make it sound as though I was salivating on her."

"The way you put your hands in her bathing suit."

Lester stared at me. "You know who you sound like, Al? Aunt Sally."

Aunt Sally? I swallowed. I didn't *want* to sound like Aunt Sally. I mean, I like my aunt, but I don't want to *be* her. I could feel my face starting to burn.

"And for your information, my hands weren't *in* her bathing suit, I was running one finger under the edge because that's a place people usually burn. And as for being friendly in a hurry, I have known Crystal for over a year."

I shut up then and tried to figure out why I was feeling so Aunt-Sallyish. Jealousy, I guess. Jealous that when Crystal Harkins had sat up finally and fastened the bra to her suit, she had cleavage that Pamela and Elizabeth and I would die for. I'll bet if Crystal Harkins was ever a spy, she could hide a secret message between her breasts, and nobody would ever find it.

Sometimes it seems to me that thoughts go floating around in the air like germs, and everybody catches an idea at once, because it was my night to cook dinner, and I'd just started to boil the macaroni when Pamela called.

"Alice," she said, "come over to my house right away. It's important."

"I'm cooking dinner," I told her.

"It'll only take thirty seconds."

I turned off the stove and walked the two blocks to Pamela's. She and Elizabeth were up in her bedroom. "What's going on?" I asked.

"The pencil test," said Elizabeth mysteriously.

"What?"

"To see whether or not we should be wearing bras," said Pamela.

"But we already do," I told her. "Most of the time, anyway."

"The pencil test tells you whether you should *ever* go without one," said Pamela, "so we're going to test each other. I'll go first."

While I stared she unbuttoned her shirt, then took her bra off. I was too astonished to be embarrassed because Pamela picked up a pencil and slid it crosswise underneath one breast, then held her arms straight out at the sides.

"Ta da!" she said, proving that her breast alone would hold the pencil there, I guess.

"So?"

"So I can't ever go without a bra. Except to bed, of course. Ann Landers said so. You next," she said to Elizabeth.

"Not *here*!" Elizabeth said, shocked, and took the pencil into the bathroom and closed the door.

We waited so long I began to think that Elizabeth had climbed out the window and gone home, but finally the bathroom door opened.

"Well?" asked Pamela.

Elizabeth's eyes were on the floor. "I don't ever have to wear a bra, I guess," she said dolefully. "The only way I could get the pencil to stay up there was with toothpaste."

They both looked at me. I decided that if I went into the bathroom like Elizabeth to do it, I would turn into Aunt Sally for sure. So I swallowed and pulled off my T-shirt, then unhooked my bra—a sports bra, if you want the truth. I don't think Elizabeth had ever seen my breasts close up before, and she turned pink and looked away, but Pamela just tucked the pencil up under my left breast.

I was about to say, "Ta da!" too, but the pencil suddenly fell to the floor.

"Did it or didn't it?" asked Elizabeth.

"Let's try again," said Pamela, and this time tucked it under my right breast and sort of pressed it there. I held my arms out at the sides. "Ta . . ." The pencil fell.

Elizabeth looked at Pamela, and Pamela sighed. "I guess she's not *bra* or bra*less*, just somewhere in between."

I was pretty quiet at dinner.

"What happened to the macaroni and cheese?" Lester asked. "There's no body to it. The macaroni dissolves like oatmeal."

"I guess I left it on the stove too long," I told him. "Pamela wanted me to come over for something important."

"What's more important than cooking macaroni al dente?" asked Lester.

We chewed some more, and I got up to put a jar of applesauce on the table so the meal wouldn't be a total waste. I sat there wondering if boys ever put themselves through the trials that girls go through.

"Lester," I said after a while. "When you were my age, did boys ever measure their . . . uh . . . well . . . um . . ."

"No," said Lester.

"Did they ever do the pencil test?"

"Take a pencil test? Like a math quiz, you mean?"

"No. I mean where they . . ." Now both Dad and Lester were staring at me, so I just came right out with it. "Did they ever tuck pencils up under their testicles to see if they needed to wear a jockstrap?"

"Where did you hear *that*?" asked Dad.

"I didn't. I mean, it's what girls do to see if they need to wear a bra."

"How do they *know*?" Lester was still staring.

"If the pencil stays up, they do. If it falls, they don't."

The kitchen was so quiet that all you could hear was the hum of the refrigerator.

"Do they teach you that in school?" Dad asked finally.

"No. Pamela read it in Ann Landers."

Lester put down his spoon, folded his hands in front of him, and closed his eyes as if in prayer. "Thank you, thank you, thank you that I was not born a girl," he said.

Dad started to smile. "Can we ask whether you passed or failed the test, Al?"

"No, you can't ask," I said.

"She failed," said Lester.

"No, I didn't! I didn't fail and I didn't pass. I was just sort of . . . in-between."

"Well, then!" said Dad, smiling.

I put down my fork. "Did you ever know a Miss America who was in-between?"

"You want to be Miss America now?" asked Lester.

"No, but can you think of *any* well-known female who was in-between?" I bleated.

"Not off the top of my head, Al, but every grown woman was once in between childhood and adulthood, you know."

"Well, it's a crummy place to be," I told him.

I decided that I would wear a bra to school or anyplace else I had to go, but when I was staying home I didn't have to. That Saturday, after I'd put in my three hours at the Melody Inn, I changed to old clothes and was outside washing the front windows as I'd promised Dad I would, when Patrick rode up on his bike. I had Lester's boom box on the porch while I worked, and Patrick pulled over and sat on the steps to listen.

"One of my favorite songs," he said.

I put my sponge down and sat across from him, leaning against a pillar. I sort of liked that song too—something with a strong beat, and every so often there would be a pause instead of a beat, and then you almost had to supply one yourself with your hand or your foot.

I was sitting there slapping my knees with the palms of my hands, keeping the rhythm, when suddenly I saw Patrick staring at me. I wasn't wearing a bra, and must have been jiggling all over the place.

My face flushed.

"For gosh sakes!" said Patrick.

"What?" I said quickly, looking down.

"Your hands!"

"My hands?"

"Your rhythm! Alice, you've got a great sense of rhythm!" he said.

"I do?"

The music stopped and there was a commercial.

"Yes, you do! Most people just do this. . . ." Patrick demonstrated, slapping each knee with the palms of his hands. "But you were doing this. . . ." And he slapped his knees faster this time, even crossing his arms and slapping his left knee with his right hand, tapping his foot up and down.

"Patrick, I wasn't doing that."

"You weren't crossing hands, but you were keeping the rhythm with your hands, and the beat with one foot. Okay . . . listen." The announcer was naming the next song. "This one is even better!" Patrick said. "Go for it!"

I didn't know the song very well, but after a few

moments I picked up the rhythm, and pretty soon I was slapping my knees on my side of the porch and tapping my foot, and Patrick was slapping his knees across from me, and tapping *his* foot. It sounded good. Not just good: great! Like tap dancing with our hands!

This time when the song was over, Patrick said, "You've got to come over this summer and let me teach you to play the drums. You'd be good at it, Alice."

"Okay, I will," I told him.

And after Patrick rode away I just sat there grinning, thinking that the girl who had failed the pencil test and couldn't carry a tune could beat out a rhythm like nobody's business!

5

Rescue

All Elizabeth and Pamela and I seemed to talk about toward the end of school was going to Chicago in July. I sort of wanted to fly because I've never been on a plane that I can remember, but Pamela and Elizabeth had never been overnight on a train, so we decided to go by Amtrak, and Dad made the reservations.

It hardly seemed fair, though, that I was going to get the chance to do something special over summer vacation, and Dad and Lester weren't. We're not poor, but we're not rich, either. I was thinking how Janice Sherman, in sheet music, let us stay at her beach house for a week last summer, and how nice it would be if she'd offer it to us again, so Dad and Lester could get away for a while.

What she didn't like last year was that Dad had gotten friendly with the woman who owns the beach house next to hers. But that was a whole year ago, and I hoped she had forgotten by now. Wouldn't it be great, I thought, if she invited us to go again, and we brought Miss Summers, and she and I shared a bedroom?

When I went to the Melody Inn on Saturday, I was

filing sheet music for Janice and told her about the trip to Chicago I'd be taking with my friends.

"How nice for you!" she said.

"I just wish Dad could get away for a little while," I sighed. "Lester too. Some place quiet and peaceful, like the ocean."

"I'm sure he could arrange it if he wanted," Janice said.

She remembered.

"Well, it's not so easy," I told her. "Things have to sort of drop in his lap, or he won't go to the trouble of renting a place."

"Perhaps Miss Summers has a cottage he could use," Janice said.

That settled that.

Janice Sherman wasn't the only one interested in our vacation plans, though. When I went over to dust the shelves in the Gift Shoppe, Loretta Jenkins asked me what the Hunk was doing this summer.

"Lester?" I said. It's hard to think of your brother as a hunk. "I don't know, I haven't asked him."

"I was wondering if he'd be interested in going camping," Loretta said.

Loretta is one of four girls I know whom my brother has dated in the last two years, and probably the least likely girl in the world to interest Lester. Not that she isn't attractive in her own way, but she's got this wild mop of unruly hair around her head like a sunburst, and I don't think I've ever seen Loretta without a wad of gum tucked away somewhere in her mouth. I tried to imagine Lester and Loretta in a tent together.

"Camping?" I asked in astonishment. "With you?"

"Well, not my grandmother."

"I'll . . . uh . . . mention it to him," I said, knowing that Lester would choose solitary confinement before he'd go camping with Loretta Jenkins.

"No, *don't* mention it to him. Promise me you won't, Alice. I'd rather do it myself. He's much more likely to say yes if I spring it on him suddenly, instead of letting him brood over it first."

"Okay, I won't mention camping," I promised.

But Lester is my brother, after all, so when he got home that evening from Maytag, I said, "Lester, I'm about to do you a very big favor, but I made a promise, so you'll have to read between the lines."

"Al, I didn't make a single sale today, I'm tired, I'm hungry, my feet hurt, and I have a philosophy paper due Monday. Don't rattle my cage. What are you talking about?"

"If you don't pay close attention, Lester, you are going to be in a lot of trouble. *Some*one, sometime soon, is going to ask you to accompany her in private to a secluded place. . . ."

Lester's eyes lit up. "She *is*?"

"Lester, listen! If she takes you by surprise, you'll say yes and be sorry, so I just want you to be prepared. Okay?"

"Why should I be sorry? Is it Marilyn or Crystal?"

"No."

"No what?"

"It isn't either one."

His face fell. "*Not* Loretta Jenkins?"

I didn't answer.

He sat down facing me. "Al, is it Loretta?" And when I just pressed my lips together without answering, he said, "If it's Loretta Jenkins, raise one finger. If it's someone else, raise two."

I raised one finger.

Lester let out his breath. "Where's she inviting me?"

I cast him a hopeless look and pressed my lips tighter.

"You don't have to tell me, just nod your head if I guess. She's inviting me to a dance."

I shook my head.

"A party? A play? For dinner?" He looked puzzled. "Can't you even give me a hint?"

"I said *intimate,* Lester."

"She's going to ask me to sleep *over*?"

I looked helpless again.

"Al, I'm going *nuts*!"

"She's not going to put it quite that way, Les," I volunteered.

"Spend the night in her room?"

I shook my head.

"Spend the night in her house?"

I shook my head again.

"Spend the night in her yard?"

I motioned to him to continue, as though we were playing charades.

"Spend the night in a *tent*?"

I nodded but motioned for him to keep going.

"Go *camping*!"

"Bingo!" I said, and slumped down in my chair, fingers trailing the floor. I had not mentioned the word *camping*.

"Al, you have saved my life. You have performed a tremendous service to mankind, namely me," he said.

"Glad to help," I told him. I had helped save two lives in the past couple of weeks, his and Crystal's. Not bad for a girl who was only a few weeks into thirteen.

I spent most of Sunday looking through Dad's books to find a poem that would "speak personally to me," as Miss Summers had put it. I read poems by Shelley and Keats and Byron and Frost and Sandburg, and thought they were nice, but nothing deep down inside me rose up and cried, "That's it!"

And then, at the end of a shelf, I found a book titled *One Thousand and One Poems*, and on the inside cover was Mom's name. My heart began to pound.

It was just as it had been when I opened her recipe file and found things she had once cooked for us, recipes written in her own handwriting. A sort of window on my mother.

I took the book over to a chair in the corner and began leafing through it. It was divided into sections—

nature poems in one, love poems in another, and so on. Here and there a particular poem was checked, or a phrase underlined. The last section was called "Old Favorites," and as I turned the pages, I saw a handwritten note in the margin of a long poem called *Thanatopsis*, by William Cullen Bryant. I turned the book sideways to read it and found, "This is one of my favorite poems":

So live, that when thy summons
 comes to join
The innumerable caravan which moves
To that mysterious realm where each
 shall take
His chamber in the silent halls of
 death,
Thou go not, like the quarry-slave at
 night,
Scourged to his dungeon, but, sustained and soothed
By an unfaltering trust, approach thy
 grave
Like one who wraps the drapery of his
 couch
About him, and lies down to pleasant
 dreams.

I don't know how long I sat in that chair, but I somehow knew that this was a poem that had helped my mother before she died. That had meant something to her, and so meant a lot, a whole lot, to me.

Had she read it to Dad too, I wondered? Had they read it aloud together, maybe? Had she decided she was going to die courageously, knowing that she had lived her life well? Whatever, I was going to stand up in Miss Summers's class, and I would say that this was a poem that meant a lot to me because it had meant a lot to someone close to me before she died. I didn't care if they put me on suicide watch or not; I owed this much to my mother.

We had to memorize our poems, but Miss Summers said they could be as short or as long as we wanted, provided we had a special feeling about them and could share that feeling with the class. As I shifted, finally, in the chair, my eye fell on a poem on the opposite page, called "Passing By," author unknown:

> There is a lady sweet and kind,
> Was never face so pleased my mind;
> I did but see her passing by,
> And yet I love her till I die.
>
> Her gesture, motion, and her smiles,
> Her wit, her voice, my heart beguiles,
> Beguiles my heart, I know not why,
> And yet I love her till I die. . . .
>
> Cupid is wingèd and doth range,
> Her country so my love doth change:

But change she earth, or change she sky,
Yet will I love her till I die.

I was crying. It was just the strangest thing! I didn't cry all the while I read the poem about death, but suddenly I was crying over this one.

I swallowed, and swallowed, and swallowed. I had found a favorite poem of my mother's, and beside it, a poem that would be a favorite of my own.

Aunt Sally called to see how my plans were coming for my trip to Chicago in July.

"Dad's got the tickets already," I told her. "We're coming on Amtrak. Elizabeth's never been on a train before, and Pamela's never been on one overnight."

"Oh, I'm so glad you'll be bringing your two best friends!" said Aunt Sally. "Get a pencil and paper, and I'll give you tips on packing."

I did what she said. Actually I'd planned to simply count the number of days we'd be in Chicago, throw that number of underpants and socks into a suitcase along with my jeans and shorts and a couple of shirts. But maybe you packed differently once you were thirteen.

"Ready," I said.

"You need to get some little plastic jars and bottles for all your creams and lotions," Aunt Sally told me.

I tried to think. "Suntan lotion?"

"Beauty lotions," said Aunt Sally. So *that's* what was the matter!

"Panty hose and scarves should be wrapped in tissue paper and put in one of those little quilted bags with sections in them."

One pair of panty hose, I wrote.

"If you have a travel case, you'll want to put all your bottles and hair sprays and things in that. Otherwise, borrow one of those little leather toiletry kits that men use," she said.

One lip gloss . . .

"As for clothes," Aunt Sally went on, "cottons are undoubtedly the coolest, especially Liberty cottons, but they're much more expensive. Cottons wrinkle so terribly, though, so cotton Dacron if you can find it, or even cotton jersey will do, but don't buy any linens, no matter what the sales clerk tells you."

Plenty of T-shirts, I wrote.

"I don't know how much times have changed since I was on a train," Aunt Sally continued, "but you should bring along any kinds of food you can't find on Amtrak. Fruit and popcorn are always safe to bring on a trip, but I'd also bring a box of dried prunes for . . . Well, travel does things to one's digestion, you know."

"Aunt Sally, we'll only be on the train for one night."

"And finally, Alice, be sure to bring pajamas. I know that modern girls don't much care for them, but let me ask you this: What would you do if there was a train wreck and you were pinned under the sleeping car and you didn't have your pajamas on?"

"If there was a train wreck and I was pinned under

the sleeping car, I would probably be dead!" I told her.

"Well, if you *weren't,* you would die of embarrassment!" Aunt Sally announced firmly.

I closed my eyes. "I'll bring pajamas," I said.

"Good," she answered.

The first Sunday of June, Crystal came over again to sunbathe. Crystal Harkins has the largest breasts I've ever seen. The largest *beautiful* breasts, I mean. Well, actually, I haven't seen that many breasts in person. I haven't even seen Crystal's naked, but they might as well have been, because her bikini top only covered the bottom half of them.

I wondered if I would ever be lying on my stomach on a towel on the grass, and a man would be slathering suntan lotion on my back and along the edges of both of my big beautiful breasts and running one finger just under the top rim of my bikini bottom. I felt all warm and embarrassed just thinking about it. So warm, in fact, that I got a glass of lemonade and took it out on the front steps to drink in the shade.

I had only been there two or three minutes when a car drove up and out stepped Loretta Jenkins. I was all ready to spring to my feet and go warn Lester when she waved. I decided I wasn't God. I couldn't be in two places at the same time, so I might as well stay put.

"How you doing, Alice?" she said, coming up the walk in a pair of pink leggings and a black halter top.

Should I lie to save Lester? Should I say he wasn't

here? I could always say he was playing cards with friends or something.

"Les around?" she asked, and I could see that the polish on her fingernails and toenails matched her pants.

"He went down the street to play cards with some friends," I said. Which was better? Honesty or saving your brother's life?

Her face fell. "Heck. I saw his car here, and . . ."

"Hey, Al, we have any more suntan lotion?" came Lester's voice as he walked out onto the porch in his swim trunks, and then he stopped dead still.

"You're back!" I cried.

"Huh?" said Lester.

"Must have been a short game," I said, turning around and raising and lowering my eyelids like blinking warning lights.

"Oh . . . yeah. Well, I made a few baskets, so it was okay."

I didn't dare look at Loretta. But I guess she wasn't even listening, because she crooned, "Soaking up the old sun, huh?"

He gave her a weak smile. "Looks that way."

"You're a nature lover, Les, I can tell," she said. "You'd rather be outdoors than in. Right?"

"Well, it depends, but . . ."

I could see that Lester was going to do himself in. Any moment now he'd agree to go camping with Loretta and wouldn't even realize it.

I slipped back inside, ran through the house, and out the back door, where Crystal was baking her beautiful bosom.

"Crystal," I said, kneeling down beside her. "Remember how Lester and I saved you from the Octopus?"

Crystal took off her sunglasses and looked at me.

"Well, we need you now! Lester is in big trouble!"

"What?"

"All you have to do is walk out on the front porch."

"Why?"

"Just do it, Crystal! Hurry!"

Crystal got up and fastened her bra in back. Then she went in the back door, through the house, and, with me tagging along behind, stepped out onto the front porch.

"You'd *love* it, Les, really! A tent right beside the lake, with just you and me and . . ." Loretta stopped talking as suddenly as if we'd turned off a voice on the radio.

I didn't stick around to see what happened next. Lester told me later that I had saved his life. I didn't know then that when Pamela, Elizabeth, and I took the train to Chicago, one of *us* would be the one needing rescue.

6

Of Heaven and Hell

I spent the rest of the day washing all my sweaters and putting them away in the trunk in the attic. It's a huge trunk that Mom and Dad bought when they were first married, I guess. You could put Pamela, Elizabeth, and me in it along with our clothes and send us anyplace in the country. About half of it is used for storing our out-of-season stuff, and the other half is used for old photos and letters and other keepsakes.

I was just about to close the lid when I saw a bit of peach-colored cloth sticking out beneath some scrapbooks on the keepsake side, and pulled it out. It was a rayon nightgown, long and straight and sort of clingy. I realized I could just about fit into it, so I carried it down to my room.

Standing in front of the mirror, I held it up in front of me, then slipped off my jeans and shirt and pulled it on over my head. It felt really strange to be wearing a gown that Mom had worn. It was too big, of course, because Mom was on the tall side, Lester said. It hugged my waist and hips, but there were baggy pockets where the breasts should be.

I was turning around real slowly, studying my rear

end in the mirror, when I saw Dad stop outside my half-open door and stare.

"Just found it in the trunk, Dad, and thought I'd try it on," I said, a little embarrassed.

"It's your mother's, Al."

"I know."

"Sort of large, don't you think?"

"In places."

"If you need a new gown, I'll buy you one."

"No, it's okay. I was just curious."

As soon as he left, I got out of the gown as fast as I could. I wondered what he'd felt seeing me in it, and how much it still hurt him that she was gone. A lot, I'll bet.

I was right, because after I'd put the gown back and had gone downstairs, I found Dad sitting out on the porch, leaning against a pillar, hands in his lap, just staring out across the treetops.

I sat down across from him, hands in *my* lap. "Sorry, Dad," I said.

He looked over as though he'd just realized I was there. "Why? What did you do?"

"Reminded you of Mom."

"You don't have to put on her clothes to do that, Al. Sometimes, just the way you smile or turn your head reminds me. But that's okay. I don't *want* to forget."

I thought about that for a while. "Do you think about Mom when you're out with Miss Summers?" I asked.

"Sometimes."

"Does it . . . I mean . . . does it keep you from loving Miss Summers?"

Dad smiled then. "I don't know yet," he said.

Elizabeth and I rode our bikes over to Pamela's the next Saturday afternoon. Her dad was paying her to wash their car, so we pitched in and helped, and when we were through, we lay out in her side yard under the sycamore and drank Cokes.

"I've decided what I'm going to wear on my wedding night," I said suddenly.

Elizabeth turned over onto her stomach. "I don't know why you always think about things like that, Alice."

"I don't always," I said. "I think about homework and Dad and Lester and what we're going to have for dinner . . . about Patrick and music and teachers, but *some*times I think about my wedding night."

"So what are you going to wear?" Pamela wanted to know.

"A long, red, clingy gown with spaghetti straps," I said.

Pamela whistled. "What are *you* going to wear, Elizabeth?"

"I don't even know if I'm *going* to marry," Elizabeth answered.

"But if you do, what do you think you'd wear?" I asked.

"I don't even think about it."

Pamela and I looked at each other and laughed. "What she should do is wear her wedding dress—the whole thing, veil and all," said Pamela, "and let her husband undress her slowly."

"*Pamela*!" Elizabeth said angrily. "I'm not going to lie here and listen to this."

"Okay, we'll talk about Pamela then," I said. "What are *you* going to wear?"

Pamela took a long, slow sip of Coke and started to grin. "I'm not going to wear anything at all. I'm going to step out of the bathroom with my hair down loose, covering my whole body like a cape. All my husband will have to do is pull it apart and . . ."

Elizabeth jumped up. "I'm going home, Pamela. See you later, Alice."

"All right, all right, we'll stop talking about *it*," said Pamela. "Honestly, Elizabeth, what's the matter with you?"

"It's just wrong, that's all," Elizabeth told us.

"But how can it be wrong to talk about something that is probably going to happen to you with the blessing of the church?" asked Pamela.

"I just don't think now is the time to think about things like that. When I'm married, then I will," said Elizabeth.

I don't know. It seems to me we should be getting ready for things like that. Thinking about them, at least. Our bodies were certainly getting ready. At least Pamela's was. I'll bet *she* would have filled out Mom's gown.

* * *

What happened next was what Pamela referred to for months afterward as the Disaster. On Tuesday, in gym, we were told we were having coed volleyball for the rest of the semester, and after we had our gym clothes on, we met the seventh-grade boys in the gym, and we all sat down on the floor together while our two coaches explained the rules and demonstrated how to serve.

Brian, who is probably one of the handsomest guys in school, and Mark Stedmeister, were sitting behind Pamela on the floor. The guys were all teasing us. When the instructors looked away, Brian and Mark would poke Pamela in her side and she'd jump and sort of shiver, and the next time they'd poke her in her other side. Patrick was sitting behind me, drumming a rhythm on my back with his fingers. It felt good, actually.

There was a boy sitting behind Elizabeth too. He had his feet straight out in front of him and was trying to worm the toe of one sneaker up under the back of Elizabeth's T-shirt. When she realized what was happening, she gave him a dirty look and scooted forward.

I don't know why instructors have to talk so long about the way to play a game. We'd all been playing volleyball as long as we could remember, but teachers like you to play absolutely by the rules.

After we'd played a game and it was time to shower, of course, the boys went to one dressing room and we went to another. Elizabeth doesn't like coed gym because she doesn't like boys to know she sweats.

"It's so gross," she said.

"If you *didn't* sweat, Elizabeth, they'd *really* think you were a freak," I told her.

"But I smell!" she said, sniffing under one arm. "As long as we're playing volleyball with the boys, I'm going to put on deodorant twice a day."

I was pulling on my socks after my shower and had just tied my sneakers when there was a scream from Pamela. I went over to the mirrors where Elizabeth and some of the other girls were crowding around her.

Pamela was holding up a long lock of blond hair. "Look!" she cried.

I looked. It appeared that someone had tied or braided a large knot in her hair in back, which was probably because someone *had*. But what was worse, we discovered when we tried to untangle it, was that they had tied up a wad of chewing gum along with it. The more we worked to untangle it, the worse it got. Her hair kept breaking off, and then little ends were sticking out at odd angles from the knot. We actually seemed to be spreading the gum around.

Pamela was sobbing. "Brian and Mark did this!" she cried.

A teacher came over to see what was the matter, and said if you rubbed ice on it, the gum would shrink away from the hair. Elizabeth and I promised to come over to Pamela's as soon as school was out and put ice cubes on her hair.

None of us would speak to Mark or Brian on the bus.

"Honestly, Pamela!" Mark kept saying. "I knew he

was braiding your hair, but I didn't see him put the gum in it."

"Don't speak to me," said Pamela.

"*Pam*-ela . . .!" said Mark.

"Again ever," Pamela told him.

As for Brian, he didn't even exist. Every time he spoke to any of us, we turned our heads away and put our noses in the air.

Pamela's mother was still at her slimnastics class, so Elizabeth and I got ice cubes and placed them around Pamela's long lock of hair while she sat on a kitchen chair and wept. The knot was up about as high as her shoulder blades, which was very high up when you consider that Pamela's hair is so long she can sit on it.

"How long do you think we should pack it in ice?" Elizabeth asked.

"I don't know, maybe ten minutes," I suggested.

When the time was up, we worked at the knot again. The big wad of gum seemed to have shrunk some, but the hair was still wound around in it, and when we pulled to see if the hair would come loose, it broke.

"Try cutting the gum out of it," said Elizabeth.

But when we tried, we discovered that we were cutting the hair as well as the gum, and there was already a dent in Pamela's long blond locks.

She was crying again when her mother came home.

"Pamela," her mother said after she'd heard the story and looked the situation over. "I don't see any way out of this except to cut your hair above the knot."

"*Moth*-er!" Pamela sobbed.

"I am so angry at those boys, I don't know what to do. Pamela's hair has never been cut since she was born," Mrs. Jones said to Elizabeth and me. "Now she'll have to start growing it all over again."

She called and got an appointment at the Cuttery, and Elizabeth and I went along for moral support. We handed Pamela tissues while she sat in the waiting room and bawled.

"I—It's like having a part of my body amputated," she wailed. "It's like losing an arm or a leg or an ear or s-something!"

When she finally got in the beautician's chair, Elizabeth on one side of her, me on the other, she decided she wouldn't cut her hair shoulder length and give Brian the satisfaction of knowing he'd made her do it, but would get a short, feather cut instead, sort of like Peter Pan.

"I w-want to save it all," she sniffled to the hairdresser.

The beautician gave Elizabeth and me two paper sacks, and as the hair dropped, we held the sacks underneath. Pamela closed her eyes and wouldn't open them at all, but Elizabeth and I couldn't stop staring. As the shape of Pamela's head and neck began to emerge, then that blond hair feathered around the curve of her head and down around the ears, Pamela looked about five years older. And finally, when the beautician handed her the mirror so she could see for herself, Pamela gasped. A young, sophisticated woman stared back at her, and when all three of us walked out of the shop, I felt as though Elizabeth and I were in the company of an older sister. A *much* older sister.

"It's beautiful, Pamela," Elizabeth breathed.

But Pamela was still in shock.

"It really is," I told her. "You look a lot older. You honestly do."

"Even better than you did before," said Elizabeth.

All the way back on the bus, Pamela said hardly a word—just clutched her two sacks of hair. But when we got to her house and she turned to go up the steps, there were tears running down her cheeks again, and she said simply, "I will never forgive Mark and Brian as long as I live, because they r-ruined my w-wedding night."

She was serious!

After Pamela went inside and Elizabeth and I were walking home, Elizabeth said, "I'm worried about her, Alice. That's the unforgivable sin, you know."

"What is?"

"Refusing to forgive someone."

"Refusing to forgive someone is the unforgivable sin?" I asked incredulously. But Elizabeth knows a lot more about religion than I do, so I had to take her word for it.

I didn't say much at dinner again. Seemed as though I wasn't saying much at *any* meal these days.

"What's wrong now?" Lester asked.

"Pamela's committed the unforgivable sin," I said.

"Good Lord, what?" asked Dad.

"She won't forgive Mark and Brian for putting gum in her hair, so Elizabeth says that God won't forgive her."

"God, who is all-perfect, won't forgive Pamela, who is a mere mortal?" asked Lester. "Wait a minute, kiddo. . . ."

I was getting more mixed up by the minute. "If you're wrong, Lester, Pamela will spend eternity in hell. Elizabeth's really worried about this."

"Hell?" said Dad. "What about Mark and Brian?"

"If they apologize, I suppose they're okay."

"Mark and Brian started the whole thing, and they're going to heaven, but Pamela, who had her hair cut off, is going to hell?" asked Lester.

By then, I was *really* confused.

"I'll tell you what *I* believe," said Dad. "I don't believe that a just and loving God would condemn *any*one—to hell. There is enough hell on earth to last a lifetime."

"Whew!" I said. "I'll go tell Elizabeth."

"Now *that* may be a bit touchy," said Dad. "Why don't you just let Elizabeth work that out for herself?"

I decided that Pamela ought to say, in so many words, that Mark and Brian were forgiven, just to be on the safe side. So after dinner I called Patrick.

"Do me a favor," I said. "Ask Mark and Brian to apologize to Pamela for putting gum in her hair."

"Mark already has," Patrick told me. "He's on his way over there now with a box of Russell Stover chocolates."

"What about Brian? See if you can get him to apologize too, okay?"

Patrick said he'd try.

About nine o'clock, Pamela called.

"Come on over, Alice," she said. "Both Mark and Brian have apologized."

"I'm so glad," I told her.

"So is Elizabeth."

When Elizabeth and I got to Pamela's, we found her in her room. Mark had left a two-pound box of Russell Stover's chocolates, and Brian had stopped by later with a one-pound box of Fannie May's. Pamela figured there was a layer apiece for each of us, and we probably each ate six chocolates before we gave up. Pamela ate at least seven.

The next morning, though, at the bus stop, Pamela looked as though she had been crying again. She had two or three pimples on her cheeks, and a real humdinger on her chin.

"All that *chocolate*!" she wept. "I will never forgive Mark and Brian as long as I live."

"This is where I came in," I said, and got on the bus.

7

A VOICE FROM THE PAST

The thing was, Pamela not only looked more grown-up and sophisticated with her new haircut; she acted it. She and Elizabeth came over Saturday afternoon, and Pamela brought along seven different shades of eye shadow and experimented with a light cream color just under the brow, then rose beneath that, and green on the eyelid. She looked like Christmas.

"What I really need now are new earrings," Pamela said. "I was wearing all those tiny little things before because I had so much hair around my shoulders, but now that my neck is bare, I need longer, dangly earrings to fill up the space."

"You could just take tree ornaments and hook them in your ears," I suggested. Actually, it was a rather good suggestion, I thought. Two plastic reindeer with ribbons around their necks would fill up all the space between the bottom of her earlobes and her shoulders.

She gave me a look, and we set out for the mall, taking the bus that goes down Georgia Avenue, then cuts over to Viers Mill and Wheaton Plaza.

The thing about shopping with Pamela is that she

wants you to look at the earrings from the front, the side, and behind. She wants to go over mentally every outfit she has in her closet and decide which ones she could wear the earrings with and which she couldn't. Then she has to recite all the jewelry in her jewelry box to see if she's buying something she already has. You have to eat a high-protein lunch and wear comfortable shoes when you go shopping with Pamela.

Elizabeth wanted a top to wear with her new shorts, so we spent another hour and a half on that. A white top, she said, would go with everything, but it would get dirty quicker, and it wouldn't look as good next to her skin until she got some tan. . . .

I don't know what it is about shopping, but I just don't like it all that much. I guess I like clothes. I mean, I want to look good when I put them on in the morning, but after that I want to forget them and concentrate on the rest of my life.

"Don't you need *any*thing, Alice, to wear to Chicago?" Elizabeth kept asking.

"I've got a closet full of stuff I never wear already," I told them.

"Then you probably need things you *can* wear," Pamela said. "Skirts? Jeans? Jacket?"

I shook my head and yawned.

We were buying Elizabeth some new socks when I happened to look into the lingerie department at Woodward and Lothrop, and there was Miss Summers, buying a black half-slip with a slit up the side.

I stared. She was holding it up in front of her before a mirror, sticking out one leg to see how long the slip was, then studying her reflection.

I wanted to rush right in and tell her it was beautiful. I wanted to say that Dad loved women in black, and she should buy it that very minute. But I didn't. I wondered if she had black panties and bras to go with it. And by the time we had walked to the Sweet Shop to buy an orange freeze, I was thinking about some of my other teachers at school.

"What kind of underwear do you think Mrs. Bolino wears?" I asked idly as we sipped our drinks.

"*See*?" said Elizabeth. "See how you always bring up things like that?"

Pamela and I ignored her.

"Purple underwire bra with lace at the top," said Pamela, grinning.

"Mrs. Whipple?"

"Cotton snuggies that come halfway down the thigh."

We laughed.

"Mr. Parks?"

"Red nylon bikini briefs."

We had just left the shop and were going up the escalator at Wards when a voice yelled, "Hey, Alice!"

I looked up, then down, and finally realized it came from a boy on the down escalator. I stared. *Donald Sheavers!*

"Who's that?" asked Elizabeth as Donald waved at me and I waved back.

"An old boyfriend from Takoma Park," I told her.

"He is one gorgeous hunk!" breathed Pamela.

He *was* good-looking, what I could see of him as he grew smaller and smaller. He had always been good-looking. Stupid and good-looking both, and I used to like him a lot.

"Come over and watch television, Donald," I used to say, and he'd come over and watch television, any channel I wanted.

"I guess it's time for you to go home, Donald," I'd say, and he'd go home.

We even played Tarzan once in the backyard, and I wanted him to kiss me, but every time he tried, I got the giggles. As I watched him step off the bottom of the escalator, I wondered if he still remembered. I hoped with all my heart he didn't.

"Let's go talk to him!" Pamela said. "Alice, I've *got* to meet this guy."

So as soon as we got off the escalator, we ran over to the down one and got on, but then we saw Donald Sheavers coming up.

"Stay at the top, Donald, and we'll meet you in lamps!" I called. When we finally got off at the bottom and rode to the top again, Donald was standing in the lamp department with a shade on his head. Like I said, he's cute, but stupid.

He took off the shade and put it back on the lamp. "Hi," he said.

"Donald, this is Pamela Jones and Elizabeth Price," I told him.

He just grinned.

"Alice's old flame, huh?" said Pamela.

He grinned some more.

"What are you doing way over here at Wheaton Plaza?" I asked.

"Just hanging out," said Donald. "What are *you* doing?"

I told him about our coming trip to Chicago and how we were taking the train. Donald spent the next five minutes telling us about an electric train he'd had back in second grade. And all the while he talked, I was looking at his arms. The *muscles* in his arms. They were *big*! His shoulders were broad. His neck was thick! His chest was wide. He was, as Pamela said, a hunk.

"Hey, Alice," he said finally. "Remember the Necco wafers?"

I explained to Pamela and Elizabeth: "The summer before sixth grade, Donald fell off his bike and had a brain concussion, and I visited him in the hospital and brought Necco wafers."

What I didn't tell them was that the day before he fell, I wished he would die. Well, not die, exactly, just disappear. I'd been thinking about that Tarzan thing, and decided I wanted everyone in the whole wide world who had ever seen me do something stupid to just sort of slowly pass away, taking the memory of my stupidity with him. But that was before Donald had the brain concussion, and then I'd prayed desperately for Donald to live.

He was into weight lifting now, he said. He was into baseball and football. Even Elizabeth was paying attention, I realized, probably because he had a little cross around his neck, and then I remembered he was Catholic too.

"You stay busy!" said Elizabeth, smiling a beautiful smile.

Well, fine! I told myself. If either Pamela or Elizabeth wanted Donald Sheavers for a boyfriend, she could have him. I would be happy if he forgot all about me. At *least* forgot the Tarzan thing.

"Well, I've got to go fill up," Donald said, rubbing his stomach. "Nice to meet you, Pamela. You too, Elizabeth." And as he walked away, he called over his shoulder, "I like your hair." Elizabeth and Pamela each thought he was talking to her.

And then, just as we started to walk on, Donald stopped and turned around. And right there in the lamp department, he pounded his chest and gave a Tarzan yell.

When I got home later, I was surprised to find a brand-new sofa sitting on our front porch wrapped in brown paper. I tore a hole in the paper and peeked underneath. It was a beige couch with a thin gold-and-white stripe on it. Very contemporary. Very masculine.

I called Dad at the Melody Inn.

"There's a package on our porch," I said.

"So take it inside," he told me.

"Are you kidding? It's a couch."

"It came!" said Dad. "Good. Lester can help me carry it in when he gets home."

"Why are we getting new furniture?" I asked.

"It's time," he said.

He couldn't fool me. I knew the reason we were getting new furniture is that we've been living with castoffs and hand-me-downs ever since we left Chicago. Dad didn't want a big moving bill when we moved to Maryland, so we left the furniture with relatives and have been living on stuff we picked up at Goodwill. But with Miss Summers coming over now and then, I guess Dad decided he wanted the place to look nice.

I was sure of it that evening when we were making tacos together and Dad said, "I'm going to be attending a music conference with Sylvia in July, Al, soon after you get back from Chicago. Think you and Lester can get along here okay?"

I blinked. "An overnight conference?"

"Yes. It's being held somewhere in Michigan, and we're staying in a dorm."

"A coed dorm?"

Dad stopped cutting up cheese and looked at me. "I'll be sleeping on the men's floor, and she'll sleep on the women's. Is that what you wanted to know?"

What I *really* wanted to know, I guess, is why Miss Summers was buying a lacy black half-slip with a slit up the side.

"Why was Miss Summers buying a lacy black half-slip with a slit up the side, then?" I asked.

"How on earth should *I* know? You weren't spying on her, were you?"

"No. I was waiting for Elizabeth to buy socks and happened to see her in the lingerie department."

"Well, I'm sure she looks very nice in black," he said, and went on cutting the cheese. "But you didn't answer my question. Can I trust you and Les to take care of things while I'm gone?"

"What are the rules?"

"To tell Lester where you're going when you're out, no boys in the house while I'm gone, the usual . . ."

"For *Lester,* I mean."

"For Lester?"

"What am I supposed to do if *he* has friends in while you're gone?"

"Same applies to him," said Dad. "No members of the opposite sex. I'll tell him it's the rule."

"Good luck," I said.

On Sunday, Dad went to an art gallery with Miss Summers and Lester was out somewhere with Crystal, so Pamela and Elizabeth came over to christen the new couch. It made the whole living room look different. Made it look odd, in fact, because there was still an old beanbag chair in one corner, a couple of lawn chairs in another, Dad's old easy chair, and a huge coffee table that took up half the space. But it was a start.

We sat on the couch, eating grapes, being careful not to wipe our hands on the furniture, and Pamela said, "I was thinking about Donald Sheavers again this morning, Alice, and wondered what would happen if two of us ever liked the same boy at the same time."

I looked from Pamela to Elizabeth. "Is that what's happening?"

"Of course not," said Elizabeth. "She's got Mark Stedmeister. Why would she want Donald too?"

"I can *like* a boy, can't I?" said Pamela.

"I see what you mean," I said.

"I think we should be totally, completely honest with each other," said Elizabeth. "I mean, it's the only way we'll ever stay friends for life. We should tell each other the absolute truth about everything.

"What we should do," she went on, "is write down five things we like most about each other, and five things we don't like, and read them out loud. If we did that every few months, trouble wouldn't have a chance to start."

"Why not?" said Pamela.

So I got the paper, and we each wrote down the things we liked and didn't like about the other two.

This was almost as bad an idea as playing Tarzan had been with Donald Sheavers.

"You go first," Elizabeth said when I'd finished.

"Okay," I told her. "I'll start with yours. The five things I like best about you: One, you stick up for me when kids tease me at school. Two, you always smell nice. Three, you serve good things when we come for an overnight. Four, you don't swear. Five, you don't smoke."

Elizabeth beamed.

"The five worst things about you: One, you go berserk when we talk about sex or bodies. . . ."

"I wouldn't if you didn't talk about them all the time!" Elizabeth interrupted.

"She doesn't do it all the time!" chimed in Pamela. "You just don't want to talk about it *ever*!"

"Number two," I said. "You're sort of a baby about some things. . . ."

"*What* things?" Elizabeth demanded. "If you're going to say something like that, you've got to be specific."

"Well, about boys and things . . ."

"Elizabeth, we'll never get through these lists if you keep interrupting," Pamela said.

"Number three," I continued. "You're always washing your hands. Four, you get upset too easily. Five, you're a little bit spoiled."

When I'd finished, Elizabeth's cheeks were bright red, and I could see she was fighting back tears.

"Maybe this was a lousy idea," I said.

"I think we should read the bad things first and get them over with, *then* the good things," said Pamela. "You go next, Elizabeth. Read mine."

Elizabeth picked up one of her slips of paper. "The worst things about Pamela," she read. "Number one: conceited. Number two: bossy. Number three . . ."

We never even got to the good things. Pamela stormed out of the house and went home, Elizabeth left soon after that, and we all sat with different people on the bus the next morning. It wasn't until lunchtime that we were speaking again.

"There's no point in going to Chicago together if we're not going to talk," I told them finally. "If we're going to get along, we can't be so truthful."

"Let's just tell each other the good things," Pamela agreed. "All the rest, we can pass on a little at a time when we think the other person's ready to hear it."

Which is why I didn't tell Elizabeth that Donald Sheavers had called me the night before to get Pamela's phone number, and I didn't tell Pamela that he had also asked for Elizabeth's. I was going to have enough problems with Lester while Dad was away, I decided, and didn't need any more from an old boyfriend from Takoma Park.

8

Poem

The week before school let out, we had to recite our poems to the class. I had been practicing every night. I'd sit in our beanbag chair in the living room and Dad would sit across from me on the new couch, holding the book in his lap. But I noticed that when I got stuck, he knew the next line without even looking.

"So live, that when thy summons comes to join
The innumerable caravan . . ."

". . . which moves to that mysterious realm," Dad prompted.

"To that mysterious realm where each shall take
His chamber in the silent halls of death,
Thou go not, like the quarry-slave at night . . . uh . . .
Scourged . . ."

". . . Scourged to his dungeon," Dad said.

"Scourged to his dungeon, but sustained and soothed,
By an unfaltering trust, approach thy grave

Like one who wraps the drapery of his couch
About him, and lies down to pleasant dreams."

One night, when I had finished, I could see the glint of tears in Dad's eyes. He tipped his head back and was quiet.

"Mom liked that poem, didn't she?" I asked finally.

"One of her favorites," he said. "One of *our* favorites. It helped get us through the last few weeks near the end, as much as anything can, I guess."

I never knew how much to talk about Mom's dying. Death is easier to talk about than dying. It's already over with. But sometimes there are things I feel I just have to know.

"Was she in a lot of pain, Dad?" I asked softly.

"No. Mostly she was just weak and nauseated from the drugs. It was the sadness that got to us—that was the painful part."

Was there anything else I needed to ask? Now was my chance. . . .

"Dad . . ." I hesitated. "Did Mom ever want you to promise that . . ." I didn't know how to say it.

"That what?"

I swallowed.

"That I'd take good care of you and Lester?" he asked.

"No. She knew you would. But did she ever want you to promise that . . . well, that you wouldn't get married again?"

"Why on earth would she want me to promise that?" Just the way he said it made me feel better.

"When you love someone, Al, you want them to be happy. And if she couldn't be around to love and comfort me herself, she certainly wanted me to find happiness with someone else. I'd wish the same for her."

"I was hoping you'd say that," I told him.

Everyone was talking about summer vacation. At the Melody Inn, Loretta Jenkins told me that she had given up on Lester once and for all, and was going camping in North Carolina with some girlfriends.

"Good idea," I told her.

Janice Sherman asked if Dad had found a beach house to rent yet.

"No, he's going to Michigan instead," I answered.

"Michigan? What's in Michigan?"

"He's going to a music conference."

"He *is*?" And then she added, "Alone?"

"With Miss Summers. They're sleeping in a dorm, men on one floor and women on another."

"I didn't ask about their sleeping arrangements," Janice said curtly, and we let it go at that.

At school on Monday Patrick told me that he and his parents were going to Canada soon after his birthday.

His birthday! I had forgotten his birthday. It's hard to remember that Patrick is a few months younger than I am, because he acts—well, sometimes, at least—a few years older. I guess his father's a diplomat or something. They've traveled all over the world. They've even eaten squid, and Patrick can count to one hundred in Japanese. He says that they've lived in Silver Spring longer than any other place they've ever been.

"You're not *moving* to Canada, are you?" I asked.

"No. Just visiting the Rockies. I'll bring you back a rock or something." (*That's* when he sounds far younger.)

I was still worried about Lester, though. I was going to Chicago and Dad was going to Michigan, but what about Lester? *Every*one needs a vacation.

"Lester," I said that afternoon when he came home from classes at the U. "Are you going to do *any*thing special this summer, or just work at Maytag?"

"Oh, I don't know. Thought maybe I might hit the beach sometime in August with Marilyn."

"*Marilyn?*" I stared.

"Marilyn Rawley. You know? The girl I've been seeing for the past two years?"

"*One* of the girls you've been seeing, Lester. I thought you were going with Crystal now."

Lester stood in the doorway drinking his 7UP. "Do I look like an engaged man to you? Until I'm engaged, kiddo, I'm playing the field, and I don't think there is any law in the State of Maryland that says I can't be friends with more than one woman at a time."

"Does Crystal know?"

"What do you mean, does Crystal know? Do I ask what she does on the weekends she's not with me?"

I sighed. Life was just too complicated right then to worry about many more people besides myself, and I decided to devote my energy to Dad and Miss Summers, not Lester and his girl-of-the-month.

Even Mr. Hensley, in world studies, had plans. He announced that he was retiring at the end of the week. The world's most boring teacher, and yet I was sorry to see him go. I'll always remember that we buried a time capsule when we were in his class, and now I realized he wouldn't be around to open it with us when we were sixty years old.

"What do you say we chip in for a cake for Hensley?" Patrick asked as he cornered some of the others in the hall when class was over. "Give him a little going-away party."

Everybody chipped in fifty cents, and Patrick said he'd do the honors on the last day of class. Maybe even buy a little party hat for Hensley to wear above his gray suit and gray tie and gray shoes and socks.

Miss Summers had set aside the whole week for us to recite our poems to the class and talk about them afterward. It wasn't the reciting that bothered me, because I could do the last verse of *Thanatopsis* now without looking once at the poem. I could *almost* say it while I was reading the one across the page from it, about the lady sweet and kind, whose voice my heart beguiles.

*Some*one, once, had sung that poem to me, I was sure of it. How could somebody sing a poem? And who could it have been? I recited it to Dad one evening and asked if Aunt Sally had ever sung it to me.

"That was your *mother,* Al," he said. "I think I even remember her singing it. It goes something like this. . . ." And he hummed the melody first, then put the words to it, becoming more sure of himself and confidently singing the last line:

"But change she earth, or change she sky,
Yet will I love herrrrr, till I die."

"Did she just make up the music or what?" I wanted to know.

"I think we had a book of old English ballads. It was probably in that," he told me.

Miss Summers started at the beginning of the alphabet and called on us one at a time. The boy ahead of me recited a poem about soldiers marching off to die even when they knew they had been given the wrong order: "The Charge of the Light Brigade."

We talked a lot about that afterward. I said I didn't think I'd ever do that. Was it courage or stupidity? someone else asked, and the debate went on so long, I figured Miss Summers wouldn't get to me that period.

I had settled back to relax when suddenly she looked at the clock and said, "We have about ten minutes left, so I'll leave it to you, Alice. Would you like to do yours now or wait till tomorrow? If it's a short poem, we might finish it today."

I wanted to get it over with. "I'll do it now," I said, and walked up to the front of the room.

Why do friends always look different when you face them in front of a classroom? Everybody looked so serious somehow. You're used to seeing your friends laughing and talking in the halls, not sitting there sober-faced, staring at you. They seemed like different people entirely, and I felt rattled.

"I've chosen the last verse of *Thanatopsis,* by William Cullen Bryant," I told them. "It was the favorite poem of someone close to me before she died, so I'd like to share it with you." And then I began:

"There is a lady sweet and kind,
Was never face so pleased my mind;
I did but see her passing by,
And yet I love her till I die."

Suddenly I realized I was reciting the wrong poem! *The wrong poem!* For a moment I thought my heart would stop beating. I could see Miss Summers out of the corner of my eye, leaning forward at her desk, but I could tell from the faces of the people in front of me that nobody else seemed to know I'd made a mistake. I wondered whether I should stop and start over, or just keep going. I kept going:

"Her gesture, motion, and her smiles . . ."

What came next? Did I really know this poem?

". . . uh . . . her wit, her voice, my heart beguiles.
Beguiles my heart, I know not why,
And yet I love her till I die."

I realized I wasn't reciting a poem that was a favorite of my mother's at all; I was reciting a poem that *was* my mother. When I started the last verse I felt really strange, and my voice sounded thick and husky:

"Cupid is wingèd and doth range,
Her c-country so my love doth change:
But change she earth, or ch-change she sky . . ."

Tears were running down my face. It was awful!

"Yet will I love h-her till I die."

I rushed to my chair, not even waiting for the discussion afterward, and sat with my hands over my face. It was burning. The room was so still you couldn't hear a thing. I knew people were looking at me. I wished the bell would ring so I could run away. *Why* had I done that? Why hadn't I stopped and done the other poem?

And then Miss Summers was talking. She was sitting

with her chin resting on her hands, and sort of looking out the window, talking in a clear, low voice:

"Sometimes," she said, "a poem moves us in ways we didn't expect, and I suspect that's what happened here. I asked you all to recite a poem that had special meaning to you. Alice did that, and did it beautifully, but the poem was not *Thanatopsis,* as she'd planned, but an old ballad, I believe, called 'Passing By.'"

She smiled at me then, and I managed a smile back. I was glad she was going to talk about it. I couldn't stand everybody leaving class wondering if I was out to lunch or something. She said that my mother died when I was four, and that this was an example of how lines of poetry can sustain us when we are troubled or frightened or angry or sad. I guess I was her star exhibit in class that day.

When the bell rang and we surged out into the hall, I was amazed that two other kids had tears in their eyes, that other eyes were red.

"Nice going," a guy said to me, only it wasn't sarcastic or anything. He meant I'd done okay.

I had to talk about it at dinner that night, though. Feelings, in our house, tend to come out at the table.

"I . . . cried today in Miss Summers's class," I said.

Both Dad and Lester stopped eating and looked at me.

"You did, Al?" said Dad. "What about?"

"I recited my poem."

They were still staring.

"What happened?" asked Lester, and then I told them how I had substituted one poem for another, and decided to keep going.

"I'm sure the other students understood," said Dad.

I nodded. "They did." It was the first time I could remember that I'd embarrassed myself horribly, yet it all came out all right in the end.

I thought Lester would laugh at me, make some smart remark, but he looked pretty serious himself.

"Something like that happened to me once," he said.

Now it was my turn to stare. "You recited a poem?"

"No. Mom had written me a letter from the hospital, and I kept it in my pocket wherever I went. And one day, about two weeks after she died, I reached into my pocket and it wasn't there. I thought I'd lost it." Lester swallowed. "I started crying in school, and just couldn't stop. Everyone knew about Mom's death, of course, so they sent me to the school nurse. I found the letter later in my room, but I never did tell anyone about it. Or about my crying."

"You didn't even tell me," Dad said gently.

"I guess I figured boys didn't talk about things like that," Lester said.

I imagined an eleven-year-old Lester going bravely to school after Mom died. He had known her so much better than I had. It must have been awful.

Dad reached over and put a hand on Lester's shoulder, then stretched out his other hand to me. I put out both hands, one for Lester and one for Dad, and for a moment we just sat there, all holding hands. Then Dad gave us a quick squeeze, and we went back to eating supper.

9

TRAIN TO CHICAGO

We gave Mr. Hensley the party of his life. Not only did he put on the paper hat that Patrick had brought to school with the cake, but he even blew the little horn that came with it and seemed genuinely touched that we remembered his retirement in this way.

Sometimes it doesn't take very much to make someone happy. All a person really wants to know is that he's appreciated and is going to be missed. There was a moment or two, watching Patrick there in front of the room, when I wished we were going together again. At the end of sixth grade, we'd decided to be special friends, not boyfriend and girlfriend. I just didn't feel ready for steady dating then, but I don't think I was any more ready for it now. I wasn't a little kid anymore, but I wasn't a young woman, either. The more I thought about it, the more I decided I had those "in-between blues."

"I've got the in-between blues," I said to Lester that afternoon as I sat on the porch with a book.

"They'll pass," said Lester.

He was right. A few days later I was worrying about packing for my trip to Chicago. Every day the phone must have rung a dozen times—Pamela calling me, me calling Elizabeth, Elizabeth calling me, me calling Pamela.

When the day to leave actually came, we'd decided to take the Metro down to Union Station, so Dad left us off around noon.

"Have a good time, gals," he called, blowing me a kiss. "Call me when you get to Aunt Sally's."

I wonder why parents want you to call when you go on a trip. It's as though Aunt Sally wouldn't let Dad know if I didn't get there all right.

We sat on the subway with our suitcases tucked behind our legs and giggled at everything. The car lurched so that Pamela almost slid off the seat, and we giggled; a boy got on who looked like Tom Cruise, and we giggled. A woman looked over at us to see why we were giggling, and we giggled some more, and then we giggled because we were giggling.

We were all wearing jeans, but Pamela was wearing *tight* jeans. I mean, so tight that there were little zippers on the bottoms to zip them down her calves. She had on a silky tomato-red shirt with the second button left undone, and copper-colored earrings, and copper bracelets all up one arm. I would have guessed, if I hadn't known her, that she was eighteen at the very least.

Elizabeth, on the other hand, had a luggage tag on her suitcase that was shaped like a panda bear. She was wearing her long dark hair pulled back in a ponytail and had on a checked blouse with little ruffles around the collar and sleeves. If I hadn't known Elizabeth, I would have guessed she was ten going on eleven.

What would people guess if they looked at me? I wondered. I wasn't chubby and cute, but I wasn't slender and shapely, either. I wasn't short for my age, but I wasn't tall. I wasn't ugly, but I wasn't beautiful, either. My hair wasn't red, but it wasn't all blond. I decided that I was a category the stores had overlooked. I was too old for the girls' department in clothing stores, but I wasn't quite junior miss. There should be a big section with neon lights blinking off and on above the entrance saying IN-BETWEENS. That was me.

Union Station, you wouldn't believe. It's huge, with nine theaters and an eatery on the lower level. It has high, curving ceilings trimmed in gold, with statues and balconies and shops and trees growing on the inside. Because we were going to have sleeping compartments, we were considered "first-class passengers," which entitled us to wait until train time in a special lounge, with marble floors and soft couches, and a bar with free soft drinks and peanuts and stuff. It even had conference rooms and fax machines. Elizabeth and I looked a little out of place, but Pamela didn't.

We left our bags with the man at the desk and went out to explore the eatery. I chose Mexican, Pamela chose Chinese, and Elizabeth got a foot-long hot dog. Then we sat there listening to trains being announced and watching people go up and down the escalators. I decided that going to Chicago with Pamela and

Elizabeth was about the most exciting thing I had ever done.

Maybe I would like being grown-up. Maybe I would love being on my own, with no one to tell me what to do. I crossed my legs like Pamela was doing, only my legs didn't look like hers, because I was wearing sneakers and socks, and she was wearing sandals that had thin ankle straps at the tops and her toenails were painted bright red.

"If anybody asks us where we're going, let's say we're running away," said Elizabeth.

Pamela and I turned and stared. *Elizabeth* said that?

She giggled. "Just for fun."

"All right," I told her.

We hadn't been at our table five minutes when four guys came along, with baseball caps on backwards and T-shirts down to their knees. One of them reached around between Pamela and Elizabeth and took the pickle off Elizabeth's plate. We tried to grab it back, and started giggling all over again.

"You come down here to spend the day?" one of the guys asked.

We tried not to smile.

"No," Elizabeth said. "We're running away."

The boys just grinned. "Yeah? Where you going?"

"Chicago," I told them.

"I'll bet."

"We are," Elizabeth insisted. Pamela was getting up to throw her stuff in the trash, so Elizabeth and I got up too. We headed for the escalator, knowing the guys would follow.

"Well, come and run away with us," another boy said. "We'll have more fun."

We shook our heads.

"So where are you going now?"

"To the train," I said.

"Sure."

They kept trying to find out our names. I told them I was Roxanne Peters. Pamela said she was Jennifer Leigh, and Elizabeth said she was Marlene Malloy.

The boys got off the escalator right behind us and followed us over to the double doors of the first-class lounge. We pressed the button. The boys stared. The doors opened and we went inside, the boys right behind us, their eyes wide.

"May I see your tickets?" the man at the counter asked them.

The guys looked at the man and then at us.

"This is a lounge for sleeping-car passengers only," the man said. "Sorry."

The boys went back out, looking at us over their shoulders. We had another laughing fit and had to go to the rest room and put cold water on our faces.

About 4:15 we followed a redcap to the gate, then down the escalator to the train platform, until we came to sleeping car #2900. I think Pamela and Elizabeth had thought the three of us would be sleeping in the same room and were a little dismayed to discover that we had one bedroom, sleeping two, and a roomette, sleeping one.

"The only fair thing to do is draw straws to see who has to sleep alone," Elizabeth decided, so she tore a piece of paper into three strips and put an *X* on one, and Pamela got the roomette.

I felt rather grown-up showing them how everything worked, the sinks folding into walls, the beds folding out of walls, and little closets only eight inches wide. Maybe I'd like to work for Amtrak someday, I thought. Be a train attendant, like a stewardess or something.

Pamela came back to our room with us, and we all crowded together at the window, tapping lightly on the glass whenever a good-looking man walked by, then ducking down where he couldn't see us and laughing.

"I'll take the guy with the little mustache," said Elizabeth, pointing to a man with a large suitcase.

"Oh, look at the one over there! Look at those buns! Oh, yeah!" Pamela cried, pressing her lips dramatically against the glass as a startled young man in tight jeans looked up.

We squealed with laughter.

"Uh-oh, look what's coming!" I said.

There were the four guys we'd met in the train station, walking along the platform and looking for us. Somehow they'd gotten down to the tracks. We dived again.

They must have seen us, though, because when we popped back up, two of them were riding on the shoulders of the others, their faces right outside our window. We shrieked.

"Excuse me." We wheeled around. The conductor was standing in the doorway. "May I see your tickets, please?"

I could feel my face burn as I scrambled up off the floor and groped around in my bag for the tickets. The boys were tapping on the glass now, and Pamela and Elizabeth were huddled together on the floor with their hands over their faces. The conductor punched the tickets and handed them back as though he ferried lunatics daily between Washington, D.C., and Chicago.

The next person to come by was our sleeping-car attendant, who asked us if we knew how to use all the controls in the room, and we all said yes. He said his name was Stan, and to let him know if there was anything he could do to make our trip more comfortable.

"Friends?" he smiled, nodding toward the guys, who were really cutting up now outside the window.

"Sort of," we told him.

The train started to move then, and the guys were running alongside. Suddenly one of them turned around, bent over, and lowered his pants.

Pamela and I shrieked hysterically, but Elizabeth went catatonic. She kept gasping long after the boys were out of sight. It's a good thing the chief of on-board services came by next to take our dinner reservations, because I wasn't sure Elizabeth's heart would hold out. She'd told me once she felt awkward and immature because she'd never seen what a man looked like naked, but now she'd at least seen a backside.

We made a reservation for seven o'clock in the dining car, then Pamela went to her roomette. When Elizabeth went down later to ask Pamela if she'd brought any Kleenex, she said, Pamela was sitting there with her ankle-strap shoes propped on the hassock, reading her magazine, and all she needed to pass for twenty-five was a cigarette in one hand.

"I'm never going to smoke, ever," I told Elizabeth. "When you smoke, your breath smells like dead fish."

"Me, either," she said. "It turns your teeth yellow."

We made each other promise that if anybody ever tried to get us to smoke, the other would step in and stop her. When Pamela appeared at our door to ask for gum, Elizabeth said earnestly, "Don't ever smoke, Pamela! Promise!"

"Who's smoking?" said Pamela. "What's the matter with you guys, anyway?"

She went back to her roomette and stayed away so long that I began to wonder what she was doing. I made my way down the hall. When I got to Pamela's roomette, I saw a man in a suit and tie, holding his jacket casually over one shoulder, leaning against her doorway and talking.

10

Pamela's Room

I turned around and raced back to our bedroom.

"There's a man in Pamela's roomette!" I said.

Elizabeth's eyes grew as large as grapefruit. "Get him out!" she breathed.

"Well, he's not exactly in it, but he's talking to her. I'll bet he's thirty at least. Forty, even!"

We stared at each other silently for ten seconds or so. I think deep down we had known that someday this would happen; someday we would have to rescue Pamela.

"Okay, here's what we'll do," Elizabeth said. "We'll both go down together and say, 'Pamela, Dad wants to talk to you immediately.'"

I shook my head. "She'd never forgive us. Don't mention her *father,* for heaven's sake!"

Elizabeth thought it over. "Okay, we'll go down and say, 'Pamela, your boyfriend, the police officer, wants you to meet him in the lounge car.'"

"Doesn't that sound a little hokey?" I asked.

"He's got to know there's someone on board to defend her!"

I rolled my eyes. "Why not just say, 'Your boyfriend,

the police officer, the one who has the black belt in karate, is headed this way?'"

We decided we would know what to say when we got there, so we both piled out the door and started along the narrow corridor. And then, around the corner, where the aisle in the sleeping car makes a sharp turn, came Pamela. Her cheeks were pink, her eyes shining, and she practically mowed us down. She herded us back to our bedroom and shut the door.

"Guess what?" she said breathlessly. "A man asked me to dinner."

I stared. "You said no, didn't you?"

"Of course not! I said yes."

"Pamela, you're having dinner with us!" Elizabeth bleated.

"Oh, it's just this one night! It'll be a riot! He thinks I'm on the train by myself! C'mon, you guys, it's just for kicks."

Elizabeth sat down hard on the couch. "I never should have come," she said.

I didn't know what to do. "How old is he?" I asked, as if that made any difference.

"Thirty-seven! I told him I'm going to college in the fall."

I was so angry at Pamela I didn't know what to do. "What college?" I said, glaring, as if *that* made any difference.

"Joseph and Mary."

"What?"

"It was the first college that came to mind. I heard it somewhere."

"I never heard of Joseph and Mary College, and if there was a college like that, I would have known about it," said Elizabeth. She would have too.

I tried to think of names of colleges Lester had applied to before he'd started at the University of Maryland.

"I'll bet you meant *William* and Mary," I told Pamela.

"Whatever," she said.

"*I* thought we were going to have a good time on the train together," said Elizabeth. "I thought we were going to play cards and just have fun."

"We will, as soon as dinner's over. I promise!" said Pamela. "It's just for laughs. You've got to pretend you don't know me if you pass me in the dining car."

"I don't know you," said Elizabeth, turning up her nose. "I don't want anyone to even *think* I know you."

"Oh, don't be so stuffy," said Pamela. "See you later, guys. He's coming back to show me his sample case. He sells sports equipment to high schools and stuff." And she was off again.

"I don't think I want to have anything to do with Pamela ever again. She just picked him up, like this was a bar or something," said Elizabeth.

"Hey, wait a minute, *he* came to *her*!" I said.

"I'll bet she waved at him from the window."

"Bet she didn't. He was probably just walking through and stopped to talk. I mean, there's really nothing wrong with having dinner with someone, Elizabeth." I was only trying to make myself feel better.

Elizabeth simply curled up on the seat by the window and watched the trees go by. We had passed Rockville and were heading toward Harpers Ferry, West Virginia.

Elizabeth was in our bathroom when the announcement came over the loudspeaker that all those holding dinner reservations for the seven o'clock seating could come to the dining car.

Moments later there was a shriek from the bathroom. I tapped on the door and then opened it. "What's wrong?"

Elizabeth was standing there, one hand on her throat. "I flushed, and you can see *daylight* through that toilet."

"So?"

"The toilet flushes right out onto the tracks!"

"Just the water. The paper and stuff stays in a holding tank."

"Alice, if you were sitting on the toilet and flushed, you would be *visible*!"

"Only to someone lying on the tracks while a train was going eighty miles an hour overhead. C'mon. They called for our dinner seating."

Elizabeth came out and was looking around for her shoes when we saw Pamela and the man go by. He was walking behind Pamela, one hand on her elbow, as though he was guiding her along the aisle. As though she might make a wrong turn or something and get lost.

Pamela didn't even look in as she passed. The man certainly didn't look at us. We picked up our meal vouchers, and as soon as Elizabeth had her shoes on, closed the door behind us and made our way to the dining car.

We had to wait in a short line while people were being seated.

"How many?" the attendant asked when it was our turn.

"Two," I said.

The attendant ushered us right to the table where Pamela and the man were sitting side by side, smiling at each other.

Pamela's smile all but disappeared when we slid into the seat across from them.

"Good evening," the man said pleasantly to us.

"Hello," I told him, and opened the menu. Across the table Pamela had grown very quiet.

Elizabeth watched what I did and checked little boxes on her order sheet to show what she wanted. After we'd done that, the man stopped looking into Pamela's eyes and said to us, "Are you coming or going?"

"What?" I said.

He smiled. "Are you on your way somewhere, or are you returning home?"

"We're visiting in Chicago," I told him.

"So are we," he said. Pamela smiled faintly and looked out the window. "Ride Amtrak whenever I can. I really like the train. As they say in the commercials, it's the civilized way to travel."

"You two are married?" Elizabeth asked suddenly. Sometimes she surprises even me. Pamela's eyes opened wide, but the man just smiled.

"Bill Donovan," he said, by way of introduction. "And this is Pamela . . . uh . . ."

"Jones," said Pamela.

"Alice McKinley and Elizabeth Price," I said.

"Nice to meet you," he told us.

The waiter came to the table just then and went over our orders with us, and when he left, Bill Donovan and Pamela were whispering together again. The air-conditioning was on the cool side, and the man asked Pamela if she was cold. He put one arm on the back of the seat, and his fingers just touched her shoulder. Elizabeth gave me a nudge. Pamela turned toward the window and smiled again.

I don't know what it was—the fact that I was far from home, and feeling grown-up, and not caring one whoop about Bill Donovan, but I looked across the table and said politely, "And what kind of work do you do?" Like I was thirty or something.

"Sales," he said. "Sports equipment to high schools and colleges. Uniforms are big in our company."

"I see," I said. And then I looked right at Pamela. "Are you traveling on business too?"

She kicked my leg under the table, but I didn't even wince.

"I'm a student," she said.

"Grade school?" asked Elizabeth.

Pamela looked horrified. Bill Donovan laughed.

"Well, now, I'd take that as a compliment," he said to Pamela. And then, to Elizabeth, "Actually, she's trying to decide on a college. What about you two?"

"Junior high," I said.

"Well, each year will be better than the last. Isn't that right, Pamela?"

"Oh, definitely," she said. It was disgusting.

When the food came, Bill Donovan talked about the joy of lying in bed on the train and watching the mountains roll by outside the window. He was drinking beer, and the only thing I can say for Pamela is that she hadn't ordered any. She was sort of picking at her steak and mushrooms, taking tiny little bites, and laughing gaily whenever Bill Donovan told a joke.

When Pamela's cheesecake came, she said she couldn't possibly eat it, that she was watching her figure, and Bill Donovan said to relax, he'd watch it for her, and then he laughed again.

"Well, I'll be glad to eat it," I said. I reached across the table and took her cheesecake. Elizabeth and I split it and ate it right in front of Pamela, and I happen to know that cheesecake is her favorite dessert. I think she thought we were going to take it back to the room and save it for her.

Bill Donovan finished eating first but made no move to leave, and when Elizabeth and I had dawdled as long as we dared, we said good-bye and went back to our room.

"If her mother knew . . ." Elizabeth said darkly. "If she acts like this when she's thirteen, Alice, how will she be when she's sixteen or seventeen? She'll be impossible!"

"She's impossible now," I said.

We sat on the couch, watching for Pamela to come back from dinner. It was about fifteen minutes later that they went by—Pamela first, Bill Donovan right behind her, only this time he had one hand on her waist.

"I'm not going to speak to her ever again!" said Elizabeth. "She's ruining this trip for all of us."

"No, she's not," I declared. "I'm going to have a good time, regardless of what Pamela does. Let's play hearts."

I got out the deck of cards, and every so often, we'd look out the window, but the sky was getting dark now, and there were long stretches of West Virginia where there was nothing outside the window but black.

We played several hands, and heard them announce the 8:30 dinner seating.

Suddenly Pamela came crashing into the room and slid the door shut behind her with a bang. Her hair was wild and so were her eyes.

"I've got to hide in here," she breathed, one ear to the door as though she were listening.

Elizabeth jerked around, her face horrified. "Pamela, what did he *d-do* to you?"

"He came in and we talked for a while and everything was fine, and then he closed the door and *kissed* me!"

I didn't have much sympathy for Pamela just then. "Well, what did you expect? You're a college student from Joseph and Mary; you should know about men like him."

"Alice, *please* don't be mad! It was just a joke! I just did it for fun! But he's not teasing."

"Where is he now?" I asked. Elizabeth couldn't even speak.

"He went to get another beer! I don't want him to know where I am. I won't go back to that room! I've got to spend the night in here. I'll sleep on the floor! I'll sleep in the toilet! But I'm not going back. . . ."

Suddenly Pamela was our friend again, a friend in need, and with her hair all wild and her lipstick half gone, she didn't look as old as she had, and I knew we would do whatever was necessary to save her.

11

Saving Pamela

"Where are your things?" Elizabeth asked her.

"I-I left them! I tried to get the big suitcase down, but I couldn't, so I just left it there. Could you two go get it?"

"If he sees us go into your room, he'll follow us here," Elizabeth said. "And if he gets in here, no telling *what* he'll do!"

To Elizabeth, a man with a beer in his belly was like a raging bull out of control.

"We'll get your bag later," I said. "You've got to be really quiet in here, Pamela, or he'll hear and start knocking."

We waited about twenty minutes, and finally I slid open the door and stuck my head out. I went quietly down the hall and around the corner to where the roomettes began, then down to number 6.

There sat the man, in Pamela's seat, holding a can of beer. I went on past as though I were on my way somewhere, but when I came back he called out, "Say, Alice?"

I stopped.

"You haven't by chance seen Pamela, have you? The

girl who was sitting beside me at dinner? She seems to have disappeared."

"Her bag's still here," I said, peeping inside the compartment.

"I know, that's the mystery. I've checked the other cars."

"Why don't you ask the conductor?" I said.

"That's a thought," Bill Donovan told me, but I could see he didn't think much of the idea. "Oh, well, she's got to come back sometime. She's probably in a ladies' room somewhere."

"Probably," I said. "Well, good night."

"Sleep tight," he told me.

I went straight back to our room, but just as I was going through the door, Bill Donovan came around the corner, and I know he saw me. I slid the door shut behind me, one finger to my lips.

We waited without a sound.

There came a knock on the door. None of us moved. I don't think we were even breathing.

"Alice?" came his voice. "Alice, would you do something for me?"

"You've got to answer!" Elizabeth said. "He knows you're in here."

I went to the door.

"What is it?" I called.

"I wonder if you could check a few rest rooms and see if Pamela's there."

"I don't think so. I'm sort of sick myself," I told him. "I guess it was the food."

Actually the food was wonderful.

"Oh." There was quiet on the other side of the door. Then, "You're sure you haven't seen her?"

I didn't answer, just held my breath.

"Alice?" came the voice again.

No answer. And finally he must have gone, because we could hear other people moving along outside our door, talking and laughing.

"What are we going to *do*?" Elizabeth wailed. "No matter what we do, he's out there waiting."

"I don't know about you, but I'm going to bed," I told her. "People always go to bed early on a train. I've got to ring for the attendant to make our beds, and Pamela will just have to hide in the bathroom, because you and I will be standing out in the hall."

It was about three minutes before we heard another knock on the door, and the attendant called out, "It's Stan. You girls ready to go to bed?"

Pamela ducked into the bathroom. Elizabeth and I went out in the hall and leaned against the windows. While we were standing there, Bill Donovan came by, smelling like beer.

"Where the devil could she have gone?" he said as if to himself, but it was really to us. "Not that many places on a train a girl could hide, is there?"

"Why would she want to hide?" I asked innocently.

"Oh, you girls get ideas, sometimes, no telling what goes through your heads," he said, and plowed on down the hall.

* * *

It was impossible to get Pamela's bag because Bill Donovan was always there in her roomette.

I put on the pajamas I promised Aunt Sally I'd bring, and Elizabeth put on hers, but Pamela, of course, stayed dressed. She curled up in a corner on the floor.

"What we've got to do," said Elizabeth from the top bunk, "is make an alarm of some kind, so if he gets the door open in the night, we'll know."

I went through our bags, looking for anything that made noise, and found an aspirin bottle, nail clippers, a roll of Lifesavers, and a metal brush. I took the laces out of both our pairs of sneakers, tied the stuff to the ends of the laces, and hung them over the handle of the door.

"Try it and see if it clangs," said Pamela.

I opened the door and found myself looking right into the face of Bill Donovan. I banged the door closed so hard that the mirror on it rattled, and it sounded as though somebody had overturned a medicine cabinet.

"It works," I said.

"He saw!" gasped Elizabeth. "He saw Pamela in here!"

Outside the door Bill Donovan began knocking. "Pamela," he called. "Hey, what's the matter? Come on out. I just want to talk to you."

Elizabeth pulled the covers up over her head.

Bill Donovan was trying to get into the room, because the handle on the door kept shaking, and the stuff was jiggling back and forth.

"Pamela!" he said. "I know you're in there! Come on out! I just want to talk. I'm not going away, so you might as well come out."

Pamela started crying.

I turned around and looked for the white button on the wall, and then I pressed it, holding it down for three seconds.

"Pamela!" Bill Donovan said again, and started pounding.

"Tell me when we get to Chicago," came Elizabeth's muffled voice from above.

And then there was another sound outside the door—the voice of Stan, our savior.

"May I help you, sir?" he said.

"Just looking up an old friend," said Bill Donovan.

"You have the wrong room, sir. You belong in number nine at the other end of the car."

"But I . . ."

"And if you come back here again, we'll have to put you off the train."

"What kind of a train is this, you can't even be friendly?" Now Bill Donovan was beginning to sound a little drunk. "All I wanna do is have a little talk, have a little fun."

"Then I would suggest the lounge, sir, but I have to ask you to leave. You're disturbing the sleep of the other passengers."

"Didn't I pay for my ticket?" came Bill Donovan's voice. "I got as much right as the other passengers to socialize with my friend. I got . . ." But the voice grew farther and farther away, and when there was a tap on the door again, we knew it was only Stan.

We opened the door.

"Don't you worry about him anymore," Stan said. "I got my eye out for him, and if he comes back, all you've got to do is ring that bell, and I'll take care of the rest." He looked at Pamela. "Now you come with me back to your own room, because you three girls need your rest."

Like a puppy, Pamela followed him out the door. We locked it after her, the aspirin bottle and nail clippers pinging together like chimes. And the next thing I knew it was Stan again, saying it was seven o'clock in the morning.

We didn't see any more of Bill Donovan. He wasn't in the dining car at breakfast, and we didn't even know if he got off the train, because it was all we could do to get our things together and find the exit. Then Stan was telling us good-bye, and we were following the crowd into the station at Chicago.

Aunt Sally was standing inside with Uncle Milt, and the minute she saw us, she stretched out her arms.

"Alice!" she said, and then she hugged Pamela and Elizabeth too, while Uncle Milt grinned from the sidelines.

"Tell me everything!" Aunt Sally said as we walked through the station and out to their car three blocks away. "How was the train trip? How were the beds and the food? Did you make any friends?"

I had no intention of telling Aunt Sally about Bill Donovan, because I know Aunt Sally. But Elizabeth doesn't know her, and if you ask Elizabeth a question, she always tells the truth.

"Pamela made one," she said, "only he wasn't a friend."

Aunt Sally stopped walking, and I almost bumped into her from behind. I tried to give Elizabeth a look, but it was too late.

"Who was it?" asked Aunt Sally.

"A man," said Elizabeth. "He got into her room."

"What?" cried Aunt Sally. She wheeled around and grabbed Pamela by both arms. "What happened?"

"He—he—kissed me," Pamela stammered.

"Is that all? Are you sure?"

"Y-yes," said Pamela, and suddenly she seemed *very* young to me. Even younger than I am.

"We rang for the attendant," I said, "and he kept him away."

Aunt Sally let out her breath, but she still had her hands on Pamela's arms. "Let that be a lesson, girls. Never talk to strange men on trains. Never let them in your room. Ring for the attendant at the slightest provocation."

"And *don't*," added Uncle Milt softly as we started off again, "tell your aunt about it afterward."

12

INTIMATE CONVERSATIONS

The first day in Chicago, we slept. It was warm and breezy, and we sat out on Aunt Sally's screened porch, talking about whether we should go see the Museum of Science and Industry, the aquarium, or the planetarium. The next thing I knew I was still on the glider with Pamela, my feet at one end, hers at the other, and Elizabeth was asleep in the hammock.

"After their ordeal on the train, what do you expect?" I heard Aunt Sally say to Uncle Milt.

But along about five, my cousin Carol stopped in to see us (she's a couple of years older than Lester), and then the pace picked up. I could tell right away that Pamela and Elizabeth liked her, the way she joked at the dinner table. Of course, Aunt Sally told her right away about the man who kissed Pamela.

"There are a lot of jerks out there," Carol said simply. "But there are a lot of nice guys too."

"Like me," said Uncle Milt.

"Like you," said Carol.

What I forgot was to call Dad, and just as we were eating Aunt Sally's lemon pie in the dining room, the phone rang in the kitchen.

"Yes, they arrived here all right, Ben," I heard Aunt Sally saying. "Physically, anyway, but emotionally they've had quite a time of it."

"Aunt Sally!" I said, backing my chair away from the table.

"Pamela was assaulted on the train," she continued.

"Mom!" said Carol.

I lunged into the kitchen. Aunt Sally handed me the phone, and it took five minutes to calm Dad down.

"Just remember that help is as close as the little white button in our compartments," I told him. "Amtrak took good care of us, Dad."

Carol was in a good mood. "Put on your dancin' shoes," she said when the meal was over, "because I'm coming back to pick you up at eight, and we'll do the town."

"Fancy?" I said, thinking of the one denim skirt I'd thrown in my bag under protest.

"Naw. Just kidding. Something fun to wear, that's all."

I sat up front with Carol, Elizabeth and Pamela in back, and we "did" Chicago—not the official tour, but the fun places that Carol knew about. Back in Silver Spring, the stores close at six o'clock, but Carol knew a neighborhood on the north side of Chicago where there were colored lights and music, and all the shops stayed open. Jewelry, sandals, and blouses spilled out onto little tables on the sidewalk. We all tried on hats—I looked great in a black fedora—and then Carol had a surprise: tickets to a tiny theater where you sat on padded bleachers while actors and actresses imitated famous people like David Letterman, Billy Graham, Joe Montana, Barbara Walters, and Dr. Ruth.

We were still laughing when we stopped at a sidewalk café later for Cokes and fries. Somewhere down the block a drummer was beating out a rhythm, and people were dancing in the street. I wished that Patrick could be there to listen. It could have been midnight or three in the morning, I didn't even know. I just knew that Pamela and Elizabeth and I were having a wonderful time.

"Is this where you go when you go out?" I asked Carol on the drive back home.

"Sometimes."

"Do you have . . . um . . . ?"

"A boyfriend?" Carol laughed. "A couple of them, but one I like more than the others. We'll see what happens." She sounded so happy, so sure of herself. How could she be happy when she didn't even know what would happen?

"I wish," Elizabeth said from the back seat, putting into words exactly what I was thinking, "that I could know what would be happening to me fifteen years from now. I mean, whether I'd be married, or be a nun, or would decide to do something else . . . It would take a lot of worry off me."

"Oh, but that's half the fun, not knowing!" said Carol.

I thought about that in bed that night. Aunt Sally gave us the guest bedroom, which had one queen-size bed in it and a daybed over against the wall. Elizabeth took the daybed, and Pamela and I shared the other.

Maybe it's easier when you're twenty-three, not thirteen. Especially if you've been married once, like Carol. I think I feel the way Elizabeth does—I'd rather know, and then maybe I could sort of prepare for it. I wondered what Pamela thought, and then I realized that Pamela had been really quiet all day. The more I thought about it, the more worried I was that maybe something else had happened in her roomette and she hadn't told us.

"Pamela?" I whispered after a while. I could hear Elizabeth's noisy breathing over by the wall. For a moment there was no answer. Then Pamela turned over.

"Yeah?" she said.

"Pamela, tell me the truth, did Bill Donovan do anything else to you besides kiss you?"

The long seconds of silence told me that he had.

"Pamela!" I said, and sat up.

"Shhhh!"

I lay back down, my head near hers on the pillow.

"*What?*"

"He touched me."

My heart was thumping hard.

"W-where?"

"On the breast."

"Did you have your *clothes* off?"

"No! Of course not. Through my clothes, I mean."

"And you *let* him?"

"I pushed him away, and he came right back. That's when I told him I had to use the toilet, and he said he'd go get another beer, and I ran down the hall to your room."

I lay staring up at the ceiling. One of us had had her breasts touched!

"Don't tell Elizabeth," Pamela said.

When we were dressing the next morning, both Pamela and I were extra quiet. I mean, even *I* could tell that we seemed different. Elizabeth knew it right away.

"What's happened?" she asked.

"Nothing? What do you mean?" I said.

"Alice McKinley, something happened last night after I went to sleep. What was it?"

"You're crazy, Elizabeth."

"We promised to share *every*thing! To tell each other *every*thing!" she protested, looking from me to Pamela and back again.

Pamela sighed. "You'll freak out, that's why we didn't tell you."

"I'll freak out if you don't."

Pamela sighed. "Bill Donovan touched me on the breast just before I got away."

Elizabeth sat down slowly, her shoes in her hand.

"Both breasts?" she asked.

"No. Just one."

"Just like that—he just reached out and touched your breast?"

"No, he was kissing me. Trying to kiss me, anyway."

Elizabeth's eyes traveled down Pamela's face and focused on her breasts. "Which one was it?"

"For heaven's sake, Elizabeth, what does it matter?" I said.

"It matters! Pamela, you ought to go to church with me and have it . . . blessed or something."

"Blessed?" I cried.

"Made whole again," she said uncertainly.

"It *is* whole!" I protested. "He didn't take a *bite* out of it or anything."

"Just the same, I'd feel better if you went to church with me and talked to a priest about it."

"*I'd* feel better if I never had to think about Bill Donovan again," Pamela said.

Every day we were at Aunt Sally's, I saw a change in Pamela. She wore less and less makeup, spent less and less time getting dressed in the morning, until the next-to-last day we were there, I swore she looked more like her sixth-grade picture than she did back in sixth grade—without the long hair, of course.

We were just having a good time being *us*. No boys, no older girls (except Aunt Sally and Carol), no men (except Uncle Milt). Nothing we had to do except make our beds and help with the dishes. We read some of the books on our summer reading list, but mostly we just talked and walked and ate ice cream.

Of course, Aunt Sally drove us to the museums and the zoo, but one of our favorite days, the next-to-last, we took the el train downtown all by ourselves, got off at the Loop, and crossed Lake Shore Drive on the pedestrian ramp to the Chicago Harbor.

All afternoon we walked along the lake, the gray-green water on one side of us, the Chicago skyline on the other. Finally we bought Popsicles from a vendor and sprawled on the grass, thinking how calm and quiet it was in one direction, how noisy in the other. Two sailboats kept an even distance from each other as they tipped this way and that on the water.

We were all feeling good, Elizabeth especially, because she said, "I decided that Carol's right; it doesn't matter that we don't know what's going to happen to us fifteen years from now, because God knows."

Pamela and I went on licking our Popsicles and thinking that one over.

"Did he know that Bill Donovan was going to come into my roomette?" Pamela asked after a bit.

"Of course."

"Then why didn't he *stop* him?"

"Pamela, he wanted to see what *you* would do! It was probably a test!" Elizabeth told her.

I decided that if that was God's idea of a test, I'd hate to get one of his essay questions.

"I don't think I believe in God," Pamela said finally.

"Pamela!" Elizabeth looked shocked. I was even surprised a little.

"I mean, I don't believe he's an old man with a beard sitting up in the clouds just watching Bill

Donovan try to kiss me. I think he's sort of a spirit. What do *you* think he's like?" Pamela asked.

"I don't know." Elizabeth squinted out over the lake. "When I pray, I think of the Virgin Mary. I see her face looking down on me, all sad sort of, and forgiving. I always imagine that when I do something wrong, she cries. What about you, Alice?"

I closed my eyes and tried to imagine God. "I guess I imagine him as about five-foot-ten, slightly on the chubby side. . . . Maybe his hair's a little thin. . . ." And then I realized I had just described my father exactly. I shut up.

"The thing is," Pamela went on, "the Bible talks about all the miracles Jesus did. Why didn't he make Bill Donovan disappear? Why did all the good stuff take place back in the Bible, and now we just have to take their word for it?"

We were quiet for a while.

"I think it's sort of a miracle that we are sitting here talking like this—that we've made it through seventh grade," I said finally. "Can you imagine Brian and Patrick and Mark sitting under a tree talking about God?"

No, none of us could. And we decided that God, whether he was a spirit or a five-foot, ten-inch man, or even a woman, had made girls a little special.

13

A PRESENT FOR PATRICK

Patrick's birthday was July 21, and I wanted to get him a present while I was still in Chicago, so he'd know I was thinking about him, even though I didn't think about him very much. Our train didn't leave until 5:10 in the afternoon, so Carol took us to a little group of shops a few blocks away to see if we couldn't pick up a present.

"How about this?" said Pamela, holding up a pair of blue nylon briefs that said KISS on the seat.

"Get real," I said.

Elizabeth thought I ought to get him some chocolates to pay him back for all the candy he'd given me since I first met him, but I wanted something different.

"What's he like?" asked Carol. She was standing in the corner of a shop, examining a bird cage. She had on a filmy blue top and a filmy blue skirt, and sandals on her feet, with loads of Indian jewelry all around her neck and arms.

"Smart," I said. "He's traveled around a lot. Sort of on the thin side. He plays the drums. . . ."

I didn't find anything in the jewelry shop or the pottery shop, and I didn't want to buy him clothes. I began to think I wouldn't find anything at all, until we reached a sort of all-purpose gift shop, and then I saw a terrarium full of hermit crabs.

"That's it," I said, remembering how Lester had given me one once for my birthday. I wasn't so happy with it then, because I was expecting a cat or a puppy, but since Patrick wasn't expecting *any*thing, I knew he'd like it.

"A hermit crab?" asked Carol, staring. Even *she* thought it was weird, I could tell.

"I know he'd like it."

"All the kids are going to ask what you gave him, and Patrick's going to say, 'A hermit crab'?" said Pamela.

"Nobody's going to ask him, and if they do, I don't care," I answered.

The clerk assured me that I could get it safely from Chicago to Washington, D.C., and I bought a plastic fishbowl with a punctured lid that fit over the top, with one hermit crab, one pound of sand, and two empty shells, so the crab could change whenever he liked.

"Good choice!" Uncle Milt said when he saw it. "I think your young man will be very pleased, Alice."

As we drove to the train station, Aunt Sally said, "Now, I want you girls to promise me that the first time a man steps into your compartment, you will ring for the attendant."

"Unless it's the conductor," I told her.

"And beyond that you just have to be very, very careful that you're not sending out the wrong kind of signals," Aunt Sally went on.

"*Moth*-er . . . !" said Carol.

"Girls can do it without even knowing it," Aunt Sally said. "Just the way they cross their legs, the way they smile, the clothes they wear . . . "

"It's all the woman's fault, huh?" said Carol. "That old argument is out of date, Mom."

"Just the same, keep your shirts buttoned, your shoes on, your bodies vertical, and don't smile at *any*one unless it's the conductor."

"Good-bye, girls," said Uncle Milt at the station. "Have a good trip back, and give my regards to Patrick."

Both Pamela and Elizabeth thanked my uncle and aunt for the great vacation, and it didn't get mushy until Aunt Sally hugged me. "Marie's little girl, almost grown," she said. "She would have been so pleased."

Elizabeth said that *no*body would mistake her for an easy mark, so she'd take the roomette this time. She was right. Roomettes have thick zippered curtains outside their sliding metal doors so that you can sort of back out into the hallway when you're raising or lowering your bed. She kept her curtain zipped all the time, so even when Pamela and I went down to see her, we had to zip ourselves in and zip ourselves out.

Pamela and I slept like logs in our bedroom. Once I got up to go to the bathroom and peeked out the window. I could see a silver river, with hills in the background, and it was beautiful.

The only unexpected thing that happened, we found out later (and which we should have expected with

Elizabeth), was that she didn't latch the foot of the bed as the sign told her to do. Sometime in the night, because she sleeps all scrunched up hugging her pillow, she felt her bed beginning to rise and thought she was going to be trapped between the wall and the mattress. She screamed.

Somebody rang for the attendant, but he couldn't get in because Elizabeth had her door locked. By the time she got herself out of the bed and the door open, there was a little crowd in the aisle outside. She wouldn't even come to breakfast, she was so embarrassed, and wore sunglasses when we got off the train so no one would recognize her.

Lester picked us up at the Metro station in Silver Spring after I called.

"So how'd it go?" he asked. "Anybody get assaulted, mugged, or pillaged on the way back?"

"You're not funny, Lester," I said.

"Carol still as good-looking as she always was?"

"She's beautiful," I said. "What's been happening here?"

"Not a lot. A man called to speak with you, Al. A Mr. Plotkin. I think he's the husband of a teacher you had back in grade school, and he wanted you to know that his wife is in the hospital."

I stared blankly at Lester. "He called?"

"Yes."

That meant she wanted to see me. He wouldn't have called unless she had!

"What's wrong with her?" I asked.

"He didn't say, but he left his number."

Pamela and Elizabeth each thanked me again for inviting them and thanked Lester too, for picking us up. And both told Lester, as they got out of the car, how nice he looked with a tan.

"Always try to please the ladies," Lester said, and Elizabeth giggled.

As soon as I got inside, I called Mr. Plotkin's number, but no one answered. I let the phone ring eight times.

"He's probably at the hospital with his wife," Lester said. "Try him later."

"Did he sound as though it was serious, Lester? An emergency or something?"

"If it was an emergency, Al, he would have called nine-one-one, not you. Like I said, call him later."

I called the Melody Inn next and left a message for Dad that I was home. Then I turned my attention to Patrick. His birthday had been the day before, and I wanted to get the hermit crab to him while it was still alive. I called his number. His mom answered.

"Patrick's gone swimming," she said.

"Well, I have a present for him," I told her.

"How nice! Did you want to bring it over?"

I swallowed. That had never occurred to me. Somehow I thought that Patrick would ride over on his bike and pick it up, but you can hardly ask someone to come and pick up his own birthday present, and even if you could, I had a hard time seeing Patrick carrying it home on his bike.

"Okay," I told her.

"In fact, why don't you come for dinner, Alice? It would make a nice surprise for Patrick, and he'd be so pleased."

I swallowed again. "Um . . . when?"

"Tonight would be fine. Say about six?"

When I hung up, that big scary feeling filled my chest, just as it had when Patrick took me to his parents' country club once for dinner. I didn't have any guidebook for how I was supposed to act! No instruction manual! This wouldn't be as bad as his parents' country club, of course; this would be worse! When we ate at the club, his parents dropped us off and picked us up again afterward. Whatever mistakes I made this time would be in front of them.

"I think I'm going to throw up," I told Lester.

"Why?"

"I have to go to Patrick's for dinner tonight."

"But you like Patrick."

"I don't like eating in front of his parents!"

"But, Al, they'll be eating in front of you! Everybody eats the same way. The food goes up to the mouth, in the mouth . . . chew, chew, chew, swallow."

"It's not just that, it's *every*thing! It's what to eat and what to eat it with and how much to eat and what to say and . . ."

"Just pretend you're here with us. The more relaxed you look, the more relaxed you'll feel."

"I don't think so, Lester."

"Whatever happens, it won't be fatal," Lester said, and took his books out in the backyard to study.

I ran upstairs to see what clothes were unwrinkled enough that I could wear them.

Then I ran back downstairs to feed the hermit crab.

I ran upstairs to see what shoes would go with what skirts.

Then I ran downstairs and ate five marshmallows to make my stomach stop rumbling.

Dad called in the middle of the afternoon. "Thought maybe we could all go out to dinner tonight and hear about your week in Chicago," he said.

I wanted in the worst way to go. I wanted to call up Mrs. Long and tell her that Dad had already invited me out to dinner and I'd just forgotten. But everything I thought of sounded wrong, and I had to tell Dad I was eating at the Longs'.

"That's wonderful, honey," he said. "Have a good time."

I was all ready by four o'clock, and then I ate a peach and spilled juice on my skirt. I had to wash and dry the skirt, then iron it. At 5:45, I left the house in my new flats, which hurt at the heels, and Dad drove me to the Longs', eight blocks away. I got out of the car like a girl going to her execution, holding the plastic fishbowl with the hermit crab inside.

I went up the steps to the porch and rang the bell. Mr. Long answered. He had the newspaper in one hand, and he looked at me over the tops of his glasses.

"Hello?" he said, and I could tell he didn't even recognize me. We stared at each other a full five seconds, and finally he said, "Is that for sale?"

"N-no," I said, my face turning pink. "I'm Alice. I'm here for dinner."

"Oh! Of course!" he said, and I knew his wife hadn't even told him. "Come in, come in! Patrick, Alice is here."

"What?" came a voice from the next room, and Patrick walked around the corner in his stocking feet, staring at me in amazement.

"Happy birthday," I said.

"That was yesterday," said Patrick.

"Well, happy birthday, anyway," I said.

"Oh, Alice, you're right on time," said his mother, hurrying in from the kitchen. "Patrick, we're having a little surprise supper tonight, and Alice is joining us."

And then the hermit crab moved. I guess I was holding the fishbowl lopsided or something, because it suddenly scurried over to the other side of the bowl.

"A hermit crab!" said Patrick. "Is it for me?"

"Yes. Happy birthday," I said for the third time.

"Hey, Mom, look! A hermit crab!" Patrick said, taking the bowl into the living room, and I realized that Uncle Milt had been right. It was the perfect present to a perfect boy from a . . . well . . . *almost* perfect girl. Sort of.

If I just could have handed him the crab and gone home, it would have been better.

Instead, I found myself sitting on one side of a big dining room table, Patrick on the other, Mr. Long at one end, and Mrs. Long at the other.

She was wearing pink silk slacks and a flowered silk top. Mr. Long was wearing a shirt and tie. Patrick was wearing a T-shirt and jeans. I wasn't dressed up like his parents; I wasn't dressed casually, like him. I was dressed in between. It was the summer of in-between.

What was strange to me was that there was no plate in front of me. I looked around the table to see if someone else had got my plate by mistake, and then I saw that all four plates were sitting in front of Mr. Long.

But nobody was eating anything yet.

"Alice, we have a custom in our house of being quiet for a few moments before dinner, and each of us thinking of the nicest thing that happened to us during the day, and being grateful," Patrick's mother said.

I bowed my head, even though nobody else did. I figured it was some sort of religious thing and that bowing my head was the safe thing to do. The nicest thing that would happen to me that day, I thought, would be walking out the door and going home, and since it hadn't happened, I couldn't be grateful. Not just yet.

As though a secret signal had been given, all chairs started to squeak at once, and when I raised my head, I saw Patrick and his mother looking expectantly at Mr. Long and the pile of plates.

"I hope you like beef brisket and new potatoes," said

Mrs. Long, "because that's what we're having. I didn't change the menu any after I invited you to come."

"Oh, it's fine," I said. "I love beef biscuit." I didn't even know what it was. Beef over biscuits, maybe. Here at the Longs' they didn't even eat old potatoes. She had very specifically said new potatoes. Maybe you were supposed to throw them out after six weeks or something. At our house we keep potatoes around even after they sprout and look like little alien men from Mars.

Mr. Long reached out to the platter in front of him, and, picking up the carving knife and fork that were lying there, proceeded to cut the meat. He laid two slices on the top plate, then two small red potatoes and three stalks of asparagus, then passed it to me. But where were the biscuits?

"Beef *brisk*-et," said Mr. Long.

"Thank you," I mumbled, and put the plate down.

He picked up the next plate, did the same thing as before, and then passed it to Patrick. Patrick passed the plate on to his mother at the end.

"Thank you," she told him.

I could feel my cheeks turning red. I wasn't supposed to have kept that plate. I had greedily set it down in front of me when I should have passed it on.

I looked helplessly around the table. The ketchup was in a little porcelain bowl with a spoon in it. The mustard was in the same kind of bowl at the other end of the table. The butter was on a silver dish, and the cloth napkins under the two forks on the left side of each plate matched the tablecloth.

Where were the rules for girls like me? Why didn't someone take me aside when I walked in the door and tell me how you were supposed to eat in fancy houses? Was this the way other people ate?

I took a deep breath and lifted my fork. The wrong one, I discovered. I put it back down and picked up the other.

"Bon appétit, Alice," said Mr. Long, and we started our dinner.

14

HOSPITAL VISIT

The first ten minutes of dinner with the Longs were some of the longest ten minutes, and worst, of my entire life.

I just didn't feel I belonged. I wasn't a relative. I wasn't Patrick's girlfriend, not really. If I had died right then, they could easily have put on my tombstone, ALICE IN-BETWEEN, and it would have fit.

It wasn't that the Longs weren't kind. They didn't ask me questions when my mouth was full or anything. It's just that everything seemed so . . . so perfect, so fancy. There were even fresh flowers on the table.

At our house, we sort of dribble down to the table once supper is on. Some of the plates match, and some of them don't. It wouldn't occur to us to pour the milk into a pitcher first, or spoon out the mustard into a little bowl. As for napkins, if we remember to put a roll of paper towels in the middle of the table, we're eating fancy.

What would dinner at our house be like if Mom were alive, I wondered? Would she have matching tablecloth and napkins? Flowers in a vase? Would she have set all our plates in front of Dad so that he could carve the meat? I didn't know, but I was miserable.

The more miserable I felt, the more sure I was that they noticed.

"What'd you do in Chicago?" Patrick asked.

"Oh, lots of things," I said, and couldn't remember a one.

"Would you care for a roll, Alice?"

I realized that Mrs. Long had been holding the basket for at least half a minute before I snapped to. The rolls were wrapped in a white cloth inside a small wicker basket. They were hot. At our house, we usually eat rolls cold. And if we *do* heat them first, somebody just stands over the table holding the pan with a pot holder and slinging hot rolls onto each plate.

"Thank you," I murmured, but I had a piece of potato in my throat, and immediately had a coughing fit.

"I'll get some water," said Patrick's father, and went out to the kitchen for a glass.

I wanted to crawl under the table for the rest of the meal.

When I had drunk some water and the coughing had stopped, Mr. Long said to his wife, "Did you see what Alice gave Patrick for his birthday?"

"No. What?" she asked.

Patrick immediately got up and brought the fishbowl to the table with the hermit crab in it. I expected Mrs. Long to throw up her hands and scream. I expected her to say, "Get that horrible thing out of here."

She didn't. "A hermit crab!" she said. "I haven't seen one of those in years. What a marvelous present, Alice."

Did she mean it?

"And two extra shells, so it can change whenever it wants," Patrick said delightedly. And then, before my very eyes, he reached into the fishbowl, lifted out the crab, and set it right in the middle of the table.

I stared. Nobody said, "Get it off!" Nobody said, "Not on the table!"

Patrick sat down again, and the hermit crab started inching slowly along between the salt and pepper shakers. Everyone laughed.

It all got easier after that. Nobody was looking at me anymore. They were all watching the crab. Whenever it got to the edge of the table somewhere, the person on that side picked it up and moved it back. Patrick even set his roll on the tablecloth. The hermit crab climbed halfway up, and his mother only laughed.

You could be rich and still be nice, I discovered. You could be rich and fancy and still be fun! In fact, when dessert time came around and I expected it to arrive at the table in flaming brandy or something, Mrs. Long went to the kitchen and came back with four large pieces of chocolate fudge cake, left over from Patrick's birthday, with ice cream on top, slathered with chocolate fudge sauce. And she ate every single bite of hers.

I helped take the dishes out to the kitchen, and Mrs. Long even let me help rinse them and put them in the dishwasher. Then Patrick and I cleaned out an old terrarium they had in the attic and set it up on a card table in his room. We spread sand on the bottom and put the hermit crab in his new home, with a few rocks and sticks from outdoors, and a lid, embedded in the sand, filled with water for a pond.

"I'm glad you're back," Patrick said as he leaned his arms on the edge of the terrarium, watching the crab.

"You are?" I studied him out of the corner of my eye.

"Yeah. I wondered what all you were doing in Chicago."

"Well, I heard a drummer, for one. We were drinking Cokes at a sidewalk café, and a drummer was playing somewhere down the block. He was pretty good. You would have liked it."

Patrick straightened up. "Listen. You want that drum lesson now?"

"What?"

"C'mon. I promised."

I followed him down to the basement. There was a family room and fireplace at one end, Patrick's drums at the other. And suddenly I was sitting on a little leather stool surrounded by silver drums with black and green sparkles on the sides, all at different heights and angles. Patrick was showing me how to hold the sticks and explaining the difference between a snare and a tom-tom, and how to work the bass and high-hat pedals with my feet.

He took a drumstick and hit one of the cymbals sharply on top. "This is my new Zildjian. Dad gave it to me for my birthday." He struck it again. "Hear that? See how long the ping goes on?" He handed the stick back. "Try it. Just mess around."

It was a lot more difficult than it looked—sort of like trying to pat your head and rub your stomach at the same time. I wasn't very good at it. I didn't sound as good as I had that day on the porch with Patrick, when we were both slapping out the rhythm of a song on our legs. But I was beginning to get a feel of how complicated it was, and was grateful when Patrick offered to give me a demonstration.

He began with a slow *rat-a-tat-tat* on the snare, gradually increasing the tempo until his hands became a blur. He moved easily from snare to tom-tom, one after another, the tone changing as he went, all to the deep beat of the bass. The high-hat cymbals parted, then clanged together in perfect time. I clapped when he stopped.

"Patrick, you're very, very good at this," I said.

"I know," said Patrick. I love it when Patrick says something dumb, because every dumb thing anybody else says or does cancels out one of mine.

When it was time to leave, and we went upstairs, Mr. Long said he'd drive me home, but Patrick said it was only eight blocks, why didn't he walk me home, and I said fine, even though my flats were making blisters on my heels.

After a block, though, my shoes were really hurting, so I just reached down and pulled them off, glad that I hadn't worn panty hose.

It was a beautiful night out, and the crickets were chirping up a storm. The moon was almost full, and there was a breeze that felt like the breeze at Lake Michigan. As we sauntered along, me holding my shoes with one hand, Patrick just reached over and put his arm around me, pulling me closer. It didn't feel awkward, wasn't embarrassing—it just felt right. I glanced up at him quickly and he smiled, so I smiled back.

Once, when we stepped off a curb, we got out of step, and Patrick had to hop so that our bodies were moving rhythmically side by side again.

We talked about school and the party for Mr. Hensley—how well it went. I told him some more about Chicago, about Pamela's experience on the train. It seemed a lot funnier talking about it than it had at the time.

And finally, when we got home, where the porch light was on, waiting for me, Patrick just stopped at the end of the drive, turned me around, and kissed me.

I had my shoes in my hands, so I didn't put my arms around him or anything, just rested one hand on his chest. And the nice part was, when he stopped, he didn't let me go and leave. He smiled down at me, then kissed me again.

"Good night," he said, grinning.

"Good night, Patrick," I said. "Happy birthday."

Then he left, and I stood on the sidewalk a moment, watching him go. I went inside, shut the door, and stood leaning against it, smiling.

I was still there when Dad came out of the living room and looked at me in the hallway.

"I *thought* I heard the door close," he said.

"Hello," I said, grinning crazily.

He took a step closer. "Al, are you all right?"

"Yes."

He waited a moment. "Have a good time?"

"Yes."

"Are you *sure* you're all right?"

"I am wonderful," I said. "Positively wonderful." And I went up to my room and sat down on the bed, grinning still.

It was 9:30 before I remembered the note about Mrs. Plotkin. I went to the extension phone in the upstairs hall and dialed the number.

It rang five or six times, and I was about to hang up when a man answered. He sounded out of breath.

"Mr. Plotkin? This is Alice McKinley."

"Oh . . . Alice . . . I just got back from the hospital and heard the phone ringing. Thought surely you'd hang up before I got the door open. How are you?"

"I'm fine, but how is Mrs. Plotkin? I got your message. . . ."

"Well, she's had a heart attack, Alice."

I sucked in my breath. I tried to imagine Mrs. Plotkin, my wonderful sixth-grade teacher, in a hospital bed instead of at the front of a classroom.

"She's doing fine, however. It wasn't entirely unexpected, as she's had heart trouble for some time, but . . . in any case, she wanted me to tell you that she would love to see you if you had a chance to run by. She's at Holy Cross."

"Of course I'll see her," I said. "When are visiting hours tomorrow?"

Mr. Plotkin told me, and I said I'd go whenever Dad or Lester could drive me over.

I sat on the floor in the hallway a long time before I got up and went to bed. *She* had asked to see *me*. It wasn't me calling her up with some problem. Not me stopping by her sixth-grade classroom at the elementary school just to see if she remembered me. She remembered, and she'd asked me to come.

Lester was taking a summer course at the university, working part-time at Maytag, but had the next afternoon free, so he drove me to Holy Cross and waited down in the lobby while I took the elevator to her floor.

I almost wished that Elizabeth was with me. There was a crucifix in the lobby, and another on the wall where I got off the elevator, and if I were Catholic, I probably would have known the right words to say to offer up a prayer for Mrs. Plotkin. Then I figured it didn't matter whether I was Catholic or not, I could still say something in my own words, so I just said, *Dear God, the world needs Mrs. Plotkin. Please let her live.*

Hospitals are scary places. They look different. The people inside them—the patients, anyway—are either worried or in pain or both. The voice over the intercom always seems matter-of-fact, but still you wonder. *Dr. Edleman, 204,* for example. What does it mean? That he's to call that extension? That a patient in that room is dying? Or is it a code that he's wanted in the emergency room?

A hospital smells different. It sounds different. Nurses and doctors walk on thick rubber soles. I wished I was Wonder Woman, and could fly into Mrs. Plotkin's room, pick her up, and fly her home again.

When I got to her door, I saw that Mr. Plotkin was with her. He was sorting through some mail, but when he saw me he smiled, and then Mrs. Plotkin turned over in bed and held out one arm.

"Why, if it isn't Alice! Don't pay attention to this silly gown, Alice. Come right in here and sit down."

Mr. Plotkin got up. "I've got at least three phone calls to make, and some forms to fill out in Admission," he said. "So you just take my chair here, Alice, and stay as long as you like."

I walked over to her bed. Mrs. Plotkin looked thinner than I'd remembered her, and her face didn't have a lot of color, but then it never had. I handed her a little bouquet of flowers I'd picked in Elizabeth's yard that morning—she'd said I could have them.

"Oh, these are beautiful," Mrs. Plotkin said. "Could you stick them in that vase, along with those petunias Ned brought me this morning?"

I put them in the vase and then sat down in the only chair in the room. When had Mrs. Plotkin's hair turned so gray? There was another woman, in the bed by the window, but she was asleep.

"How are you?" I asked.

"Thoroughly disgusted with myself," Mrs. Plotkin said, "and bored. The thing about being in a hospital, dear, is you get bored. We don't have to whisper. My roommate is not only asleep, but she's deaf as well."

"I was really worried when I got the message."

"Well, don't be. If I had to have a heart attack, I guess, summer is the best time to have one, because I fully expect to be back in my classroom this fall. Ned tells me that your brother said you were in Chicago visiting your aunt. I want to hear all about it, so start at the beginning."

I told her everything. Even about Pamela being kissed in her roomette. About Elizabeth folding up into the wall. And then, because she was listening so intently and seemed to care so much, I told her about dinner at the Longs' and how Patrick had kissed me afterward, so I guessed maybe we were "going together" again.

Mrs. Plotkin smiled up at the ceiling. "I can remember *my* first kiss," she said, "only I was older than you are, Alice. Probably close to seventeen . . ."

I didn't tell her this wasn't my *first* kiss, because I wanted to hear about hers.

"The nice part about it was that it was unexpected; I didn't have to worry about it beforehand. Just a nice evening with a nice boy, and he kissed me before we even reached the porch. Do you know, I still can remember the smell of honeysuckle that night. It's just the strangest thing. I never smell honeysuckle without remembering that kiss."

This must be the way it is when you have a mother, I thought. You tell her things and she tells you things, and it helps you prepare for what's coming.

"What I *really* wanted you to come by for was this," she said at last, sitting up on one elbow and reaching across to a shoe box on her nightstand. "Ned has been bringing me boxes and folders and things to sort, and he brought in this old box of photographs. Do you still have the ring I gave you?"

"Yes," I told her. I will have that ring for the rest of my life. On the last day of sixth grade, when all of the other students were gone, Mrs. Plotkin had given me a very old ring with a large green stone in it. The silver was worn, and the stone had a tiny chip on one side, but it had belonged to her great-grandmother, who had passed it down to her. She was supposed to pass it on to *her* daughter, but since she had no children, not even a niece, she'd decided to give it to me.

"Well, I found this old photograph of my great-grandmother—*two* photos, actually—and I thought you might like to have one. Since you have the ring, you know. To know that it once belonged to her, and then to my grandmother, then my mother, and then to me . . ."

I sat very still, looking at the picture of her great-grandmother. In this photo she must have been a woman of about twenty, very serious, in a tight satin dress that had a high neck and ruffle, and a little satin hat. There was something about her mouth that looked like Mrs. Plotkin's mouth—also something about the ears. You could definitely tell they were related. I wished I had worn the ring to the hospital that day.

"I'll keep it forever, along with the ring," I told her.

When her husband came back finally, I got up to leave. I was just going to sort of squeeze her hand, but I bent down and kissed her on the forehead.

"I'll see you again, Alice," she said, "and it was simply wonderful having you come to visit. Just wonderful."

On the elevator going down, I was holding the picture out in front of me, and a woman said, "That's a beautiful picture. It looks very old. Who is she?"

"My great-great grandmother," I said, and decided it was close enough to the truth.

15

HOLDING THE FORT

Dad and Miss Summers flew to the music conference in Michigan the following day.

"You and Lester hold the fort now," Dad said, just before he got in the cab.

I was getting good at keeping things under control, I decided. There were about a dozen times over the summer I could have freaked out, but hadn't, so that was progress.

I was also doing well with my summer reading list. The librarian had given out one for girls and one for guys, and already I was deep into the problems of other girls, which made mine seem pretty small. I had read *Sydney Herself,* and *Izzy, Willy Nilly,* and still had *After the Rain; Like Seabirds Flying Home; Jacob Have I Loved;* and *Send No Blessings* yet to go. Most of the girls in the books were older than I am, and it was like reading the diaries of older sisters, knowing that if they could get through the problems in *their* lives, I could get through mine.

Except that, when I thought about it, I didn't have so many problems right then. I was lying out on a blanket under a tree, reading, when suddenly I put my book down and realized that I was sort of between problems. I didn't stick pencils up my nose and pretend I was an elephant as I had back in third grade, or play Tarzan on a raft with Donald Sheavers as I had in fourth, and I didn't have love problems like Lester, either. Maybe there *was* something nice about being in-between for a while.

I began to sing, if you can call it that, one of the songs from *Porgy and Bess*:

"Oh, I got plenty o' nuttin,'
An' nuttin's plenty fo' me. . . ."

The sky had clouded up, and I felt a few heavy drops on my legs, so I gathered up my blanket and books and went inside. I'd just stepped in the back door, when I heard voices coming from above. I stopped and listened. It didn't sound like the radio. I went down the hall to the bottom of the stairs and listened some more. It was Lester and a woman up in his bedroom. Marilyn or Crystal?

Now what should I do? Dad had specifically told us both that we weren't to have anyone in while he was gone. Patrick had already called and was coming over the next day, but we'd sit on the porch. I certainly wouldn't invite him up to my room.

I went halfway up, trying to think. There were murmured voices, then a soft rustle, like the crinkling of a paper bag. More murmured voices, a giggle, a rustle.

Talk . . . giggle . . . talk . . . rustle . . . talk . . . giggle . . . talk . . . rustle . . .

I'll admit I don't know much about love, but what could they be doing with a paper bag? It was embarrassing. I *had* to get them out of there.

I went back down to the kitchen and got an aluminum pie pan, then sat on the bottom step, with the pan on my knees, and began tapping out a rhythm. Every so often I hit the wall with one hand for the beat. *Thump, ta ta, thump, ta ta* . . . and when that didn't get results, I started to sing as loudly as I could:

"Oh, I got plenty o' nuttin',
An' nuttin's plenty fo' me.
I got no car, got no mule, I got no misery. . . ."

Lester's bedroom door opened in a hurry. "Good grief, Al!" he cried.

I looked up.

Marilyn. She was a short, slender woman with long brown hair, standing there, fully dressed in a white cotton skirt and blouse, with green-and-blue dangly earrings. She was eating a bag of popcorn. I was so relieved to see the popcorn I hardly knew what to say.

"Hi, Alice," she said. "I'm absolutely starved, and I just dropped by to invite Les to dinner. You're invited too."

"Me?"

"Why not?" said Lester. "It's my turn to cook tonight, and this will save me the trouble. Let's go."

"There's a Greek restaurant I've been wanting to try. I'm really hungry for spanakopita," Marilyn told me.

I didn't know what spanakopita was, but suddenly I was hungry for it too.

"I'm ready," I said, and we all went outside.

It was nice, come to think of it—being invited. I didn't have to put on flats and panty hose, but I could wear dangly earrings, just like Marilyn. I didn't have to worry about pronouncing things right on the menu, but I knew I could carry on an intelligent conversation. I didn't know what was happening with Crystal, and I didn't know how Dad and Miss Summers were getting along in Michigan, but I was holding the fort here in Silver Spring, just as Dad said to, and doing a pretty good job of it.